ONE WAY TO LOVE

Glenna Finley

There are many ways to love—
"and every single one of them is right."
—KIPLING

A SIGNET BOOK
NEW AMERICAN LIBRARY
TIMES MIRROR

Copyright © 1982 by Glenna Finley

SIGNET TRADEMARK REG. U.S. PAT. OFF. AND FOREIGN COUNTRIES
REGISTERED TRADEMARK—MARCA REGISTRADA
HECHO EN CHICAGO, U.S.A.

SIGNET, SIGNET CLASSICS, MENTOR, PLUME, MERIDIAN AND NAL
Books are published by The New American Library, Inc.,
1633 Broadway, New York, New York 10019

First Printing, March, 1982

1 2 3 4 5 6 7 8 9

PRINTED IN THE UNITED STATES OF AMERICA

"GET IN THE HOUSE BEFORE I FORGET THE THINGS MY MOTHER TAUGHT ME ABOUT HOW TO TREAT A LADY!"

Gwen could feel her heart thumping in her breast like a long-distance runner's. She tried desperately to control her breathlessness so he wouldn't know the havoc he was causing, but she managed to challenge his ultimatum. "And if I don't?"

"Then," he said, reaching out and pulling her to him in one decisive moment, "you'll be in big trouble. Do you need convincing?" he added, a moment before his lips came down on hers . . .

For

J. D. F.

Chapter One

As an earthly Eden, the Desert Villas resort was missing a few requisites, no matter what the brochure on posh Palm Springs watering holes claimed.

There were only three strategically placed cottages and each was a two-story stucco structure with a tiled roof, considerably more modest than some of the other homes in that neighborhood. Those rated in the "estate" category and could have housed exiled royalty in former days. With current mortgage rates, most exiled bluebloods couldn't have made the down payment let alone pay monthly maintenance. In addition to the lavish buildings, some of the estates even boasted artificial lakes which served as modern moats, presumably adding to the joy of the local tax assessor when he made his rounds. In contrast, the residents of the Desert Villas had to share a single swimming pool—although it was a gleaming, free-form affair that fit splendidly into the manicured grounds.

In most resorts, such a pool would have rated more than a mention, but swimming pools were so commonplace in Palm Springs real estate that residents regarded them much the same way as Boston ladies regarded their hats; one didn't buy them, one simply had them.

When Gwen Lawson had driven through the center of Palm Springs that forenoon before arriving at the Desert Villas she'd discovered that California resort dwellers took other things for granted besides swimming pools. There was a shopping area on East Palm Canyon Drive which supplied everything from sneakers to chandeliers for a price. She had the feeling that if she'd asked for dancing girls to go with the zebra rug and brass hookah on display in one window, they would have been sent out on the afternoon delivery, along with quail's eggs and caviar for the feast. Even the neighboring shopping center had a southern California touch; the liquor store and health bar shared the same entrance while a loan office and a Center for Interacting Meditation were just next door.

"Definitely a place for all seasons," Gwen murmured later that day as she walked over to the edge of the villas' swimming pool and stared down at its calm blue surface. There wasn't a floating leaf or bug to mar its perfection—probably due to the efforts of a tall rangy man wearing a T-shirt and some disreputable khaki shorts at the other end of the pool. At that moment, he was putting a long-handled dip net into a cart, but he straightened to survey her calmly before resuming his work.

His disinterest was so patent that Gwen's cheeks took on added color. While she hadn't made a conscious effort to attract his attention, it was a different reaction than she usually encountered. Her feminine assets, distributed over a trim figure, had been very much in evidence ever since her late teens. And even though she'd celebrated her twenty-fourth birthday a few weeks before, things hadn't changed. Her sandy hair had been recently cut short and she wore it brushed softly back, its easy style complementing her finely chiseled features. Thick lashes framed a pair of beautiful brown eyes that, in turn, surmounted a small straight nose and curving lips. Just then, however, the lips were firm and her chin was at a dangerous angle.

Her aunt, emerging from the cottage onto the patio next to the pool, recognized the warning signs and her own eyebrows shot up. "Trouble in paradise so soon?" she asked in crisp tones which matched her spare, but elegantly clad, figure.

"Aunt Pearl! You startled me. I was thinking of something else."

"The way you looked, I was ready to lock up the kitchen knives." Pearl Harris glanced around the quiet scene in front of her. The caretaker was disappearing around the corner of the villa and her glance narrowed thoughtfully. "Problems?" she asked Gwen drily.

"The man didn't even give me a second glance." And when her aunt merely waited, Gwen shook her head. "I'm tired, that's all. It was a long drive. Let's

3

have a swim before we unpack—unless that pool maintenance man objects."

"Why on earth should he?" Her aunt reached into the pocket of her linen blazer jacket for her sunglasses and put them on. "Do you suppose he's the one we ask to move that umbrella table out onto the patio?"

"We could try." Gwen rubbed her forehead and wished that she'd worn a skirt rather than the dacron knit slacks which had seemed so sensible early that morning up in the mountains that edged the Mojave. "What did the landlord say in his letter about caretakers?"

"Mr. Fletcher?" Pearl Harris pursed her thin lips as she tried to remember. "I don't think he mentioned one. It's strange he hasn't appeared—or left a note or something. You wrote saying that we'd arrive today, didn't you?"

"Loud and clear." Gwen looked pointedly back at the corner of the adjacent cottage where the maintenance man had disappeared. "It appears our caretaker has now gone forever. Probably on an extended coffee break."

"More likely a late lunch. Well, we can always drag that umbrella table out ourselves. After a Montana winter, I'm not used to this kind of weather in March."

Gwen smiled in agreement. "It does make that long drive south worthwhile."

"I just hope this vacation lease was a good idea. We might have been more comfortable at that place where the Matlocks stayed last year."

Gwen shoved her hands in her pants pockets.

"From the report I heard, it was one long round of cocktail parties and golf tournaments."

"I don't know why you sound so scornful." Pearl peered sharply over her sunglasses. "That's what vacations are for."

"Sorry, love. I'll be more sociable after I change out of these clothes. If Adonis comes into view—whistle. I'll lean out the window and get him cracking for us." She tossed a grin over her shoulder. "With both bedrooms overlooking the pool, we'll have a front seat for the action."

She spared an approving look as she entered the villa's long rectangular living room, its TV alcove at one end opposite a smoky mirrored fireplace wall. Decorators had chosen a restful color scheme with walls of beige and a carpet of soft gray. Most of the upholstered pieces were covered in slate-blue linen, but a built-in corner sectional in the TV alcove featured a contemporary beige and blue print. The overall effect provided a muted retreat from the bright desert sunshine outside.

Upstairs, the two bedrooms with adjoining baths utilized the same general color scheme. Gwen's room boasted a king-sized bed with a deep blue shantung spread plus teak bureaus lining one entire wall. The elusive Mr. Fletcher couldn't be faulted on villa furnishings and decor, she thought as she rummaged for a swimsuit in the bottom bureau drawer. And maybe she should be thankful that he wasn't around making them sign for possible damage claims and all the other impedimenta that went with a short-term lease.

Such discussions were the last thing her aunt needed after surgery and a hospital stay. Since Pearl had served as both mother and father after Gwen had been orphaned as a toddler, she was determined that her aunt should have a pleasant convalescence in the sunshine that the doctor recommended. A neighbor told them about the Desert Villas and a long-distance phone call promptly brought a letter of confirmation from the manager. It only needed a hefty deposit to finalize the proceedings. After that, it hadn't taken much persuasion to make Pearl leave her Montana ranch, which adjoined Gwen's property near the Canadian border where winter was lingering stubbornly.

The drive south had been pleasant, but it was with relief that they'd finally pulled into Palm Springs earlier in the day. After stopping for lunch in town, they'd eventually made their way to the villa.

And certainly everything had been as advertised, Gwen had to admit. The landlord hadn't promised any staff to greet them on arrival. Their villa door had been left unlocked, as promised, and two keys were on the front hall table.

It was just a minor nuisance to go down and wrestle with the umbrella table, she conceded. Once she moved that and pulled some of the lounges under cover on the patio so her aunt could take an afternoon siesta in the shade, she'd jump in that glorious pool and concentrate on important things. Like whether they should splurge on steaks for dinner or settle for a salad and dessert.

Gwen stared thoughtfully at her one-piece swimsuit and her bikini which was beside it in the bureau drawer, recalling the sunning possibilities on the patio. Certainly there weren't any potted palms to hide behind if the occupants of the other two villas descended on the poolside. On the other hand, if she wanted to acquire a tan, the blue and white print bikini was the sensible thing to wear.

After she got into it a few minutes later, she surveyed her reflection in the full-length mirror on the bathroom door and raised her eyebrows at the expanse of bare skin. It was fortunate that she'd brought an ankle-length wraparound skirt to provide cover getting to the poolside. She slipped into that and picked up a towel. Shoving her sunglasses to the top of her head, she left the bedroom and went down the stairs.

There was a rattle of ice cubes in the kitchen and she paused in the doorway to survey her aunt getting a soft drink from the refrigerator.

"If you'll make that two," Gwen told her, "I'll go move the table to put them on."

"I'll be happy to make it two," Pearl agreed, "but that table's too heavy for you to be dragging around. And you're really not dressed for it—unless things have changed since my day."

Gwen grinned and pirouetted in the doorway. "Madame doesn't like?"

"There isn't enough to dislike. I just hope that the men around this place don't suffer from high blood pressure. That outfit's a menace."

"If you think I should change it . . ."

"Don't be absurd," her aunt cut in crisply. "Just be prepared to make some new friends."

"Right now, I'd settle for anybody with muscles. If that swimming pool man comes back, point him toward the storage shed."

Gwen went around the outside of the villa and opened the door of a small utility building which adjoined their garage. There were two lounges with pads under plastic covers along one wall plus a rattan umbrella table with aluminum folding legs. The umbrella itself was hanging from a hook above it, shrouded in a protective plastic bag. Gwen frowned and went over to heft it experimentally. Who would ever have thought that those umbrellas were so darned heavy! Well, there was nothing for it but a solid heave to move it up and off the hook. Once she lowered it to the ground, she could get a decent grasp on it to carry it around by the pool.

It only took an instant to realize that she had on the wrong outfit for the job. The flimsy jersey bra of the bikini slid upward just as Gwen, by dint of an undignified heave that landed her nose against the wallboard, managed to get the umbrella unhooked. But as it slithered downward in her arms her real trouble developed. The fine chain which apparently adjusted the tilt of the umbrella caught the metal buckle which held the front of her bikini bra together. The lightweight jersey promptly reversed its trend; instead of going up, it went decidedly down, with the full weight of the umbrella acting as an anchor.

"Damn!" Gwen fumed and clutched the bra with one hand to pull it back into place while the umbrella descended toward her bare toes. She abandoned modesty for necessity and clutched the umbrella with both arms once again, trying to find an empty spot to deposit it on the cement floor.

Even as flustered as she was, there was no missing

the sound of smothered laughter from the doorway. Her head jerked in alarm just as a masculine voice asked, "Need some help?"

"I certainly do . . ." Gwen began, only to break off as she remembered that the umbrella she was clutching to her breast was the only covering for that part of her body just then. "No! Don't take it away!" The last was an alarmed squeak as he came over and reached for her plastic-wrapped bundle.

"Why not, for God's sake?" He got a firm clasp on the umbrella, obviously intent on relieving her of her burden. "You're going to be covered with dust for one thing and for another . . ."

This time it was *his* voice that trailed off as he caught a glimpse of her problem.

Gwen took advantage of his hesitation to yank the umbrella back against her. For the first time, she noted that their pool maintenance man had changed into a pair of lightweight beige slacks topped with a good-looking rust sport shirt. His dark hair was still damp from a recent shower and there was the faintest aura of lime after-shave from his tanned skin. He didn't attempt to hide the amusement in his gray eyes as he acknowledged her plight. "You appear to be in a dilemma."

His comment was the last straw so far as Gwen was concerned. "I wouldn't be if you'd been around when I needed you. Didn't your employer bother to tell you we were arriving today?"

His dark eyebrows drew together.

"Mr. Fletcher—our missing landlord," she went on impatiently. "Or do you just work for a pool service? Not that it matters right now."

He nodded gravely. "First things first. Why don't I close my eyes and hang onto this umbrella while you make some repairs." The last two words came out after a tactful pause.

"That would help." Gwen waited just long enough to see his plan go in effect before she made a grab to pull her bra again into place. Unfortunately, the decorative buckle clasp at the front obviously hadn't been designed to cope with sun furniture. She struggled to bend it back into shape so the catch would function and almost let go of the whole thing when her rescuer spoke again.

"Having trouble?"

Her accusing glance shot upward but his eyelids appeared firmly shut. She let her own gaze linger on his tanned face long enough to note that he possessed incredibly thick lashes. By comparison her own sandy ones couldn't compete. How ridiculous for a man to have such things, she fumed. At that moment, the lashes in question went up and his amused glance met hers.

As she opened her mouth to protest, he said, "You didn't answer me. What was I supposed to do?"

Gwen could feel her cheeks grow hot as his eyes slipped down to where her hands still clutched the front of her bikini. "I'd suggest that you move that umbrella out beside the pool," she said, trying to sound crisp and uncaring. "My aunt would like some shade."

"Mrs. Harris?" he asked, remaining exactly where he was. "She's the one who sent me in here to give you a hand."

"Well, then . . ."

"Which I would have been glad to do." He didn't attempt to hide the laughter in his deep voice then. "Except that I'd probably have gotten my face slapped if I'd tried."

"You didn't have to take her literally—" Gwen began before she realized that he'd been leading her on again. "Very funny. Just take that miserable umbrella, Mr. whatever your name is. I'm going to change."

"I'd recommend another locale." He hoisted the umbrella obediently under one arm. "Incidentally, my name is Fletcher. Lance Fletcher."

She stared up at him in dismay as the name registered. "You mean *that* Mr. Fletcher. Our missing landlord?"

"I wasn't missing. I just thought I'd better shave and put on a shirt before I came to pay my respects. There's nothing wrong with that, is there?"

"Of course not." Gwen's clutch on the material at her bosom tightened. She should have known that he'd put her on the defensive. He was just that type. Tall, assured, and probably the kind of man who hadn't made a mistake since he'd turned thirty—although that couldn't have been long ago. Her mental meanderings came to an abrupt halt as his other comment registered. "What's with this 'other locale' bit?"

He took a deep breath and said in slow kindly fashion, like someone addressing a slightly demented character, "I wouldn't recommend doing any more repairs on that bikini in this place. The tenants from the other villa occasionally come in here for an extra lounge pad—"

"You don't have to worry," she cut in. Her voice was so tight with annoyance that it sounded thready to her own ears. She started to gesture for emphasis and remembered it would be disastrous before he could even start to grin. "Oh, really!" she gasped, and stomped out into the sunshine.

It didn't help that she stubbed her toe on the edge of the door as she swept past him and saw his chest start to heave with laughter before she could get beyond range.

She *did* have enough presence of mind to slip in the side door to the kitchen and noted thankfully that it was deserted. The sound of voices from the poolside showed where the occupants of the Desert Villas were gathering. Gwen peered carefully around the kitchen curtain to confirm that her landlord was finding his way to the pool area with the miserable umbrella.

Not waiting to identify any of the others, she slipped through the quiet living room and up to her bedroom again. She didn't waste any time in tearing off the offending bikini and its coverup skirt. Her recent experience had shaken her enough that she darted back to lock the bedroom door, although she knew it was a foolish gesture. Lance Fletcher wasn't the type to come wandering into the house without an invitation.

Gwen hesitated in the process of pulling on a pair of pale yellow linen slacks as she suddenly wondered exactly how long he'd stood in the door of that utility hut before he'd announced his presence. Stood there and undoubtedly enjoyed her struggle. "Damn the man!" she muttered and reached for a long-sleeved blouse. Her suntan would have to wait—she'd furnished enough of a floor show for one day!

The damaged bikini was swept back into the drawer and Gwen knew for a certainty that it would eventually go back into her suitcase unworn. It would take months before she'd be able to look at that twisted clasp on the bra without wincing.

For an instant, she thought about just going down to the kitchen and making herself a cup of coffee, skipping the outdoor gathering altogether. Then she chided herself for surrendering so meekly. She applied a bright red lipstick as additional armor and put on her sunglasses before going down the stairs once again. At that rate, she'd have a path worn on the carpet before they left—which would really give Mr. Fletcher an excuse to claim damages.

Her landlord didn't appear to have anything so dastardly on his mind when she emerged into the sunlight of their patio.

He'd erected the umbrella table and surrounded it with some comfortable rattan chairs. Her aunt was sitting in one of them, very much at ease as she chatted with him, lounging at her side. He smiled and got to his feet as Gwen advanced, as did another man who was sitting across the table from them. The only person in the group who wasn't smiling just then was a platinum blonde woman stretched out on a lounge nearby. She was wearing such a minuscule bikini that Gwen gulped and then hastily turned her attention back to the table again as her aunt said, "Gwen, dear, I know you've already met Lance . . ."

Was there an undertone of amusement in her crisp tones, as well? Gwen wondered about it even as she muttered something incomprehensible and kept her gaze averted from her landlord's thoughtful appraisal.

"And this is Mr. Brown . . ." her aunt was going on.

"Stanton Brown." The man across the table extended his hand. "I'm your neighbor on the other side."

"Along with Miss Crane," Pearl Harris continued, imperturbably nodding toward the blonde on the nearby lounge as Brown sat down again.

The blonde raised her head then, and pulled her sunglasses down her nose to peer over them. "Sherry gets my attention faster than Miss Crane," she drawled, as she subjected Gwen's slacks and shirt to an intent scrutiny. "Doesn't the heat bother you in all those clothes?"

Stanton Brown had been smoothing his thinning hair, but he brought his hand down abruptly to slap the top of the table. "You know what I've told you about shooting off your . . ." he began, and then stopped as he saw the startled faces around him. His already florid complexion turned even redder as he mumbled, "Sorry. My secretary gets carried away sometimes. Isn't that right, Sherry?"

The blonde surged to her feet with a fluid motion and came over to rest a cautious hand on his shoulder. "Of course, Stan. I didn't mean anything out of line, Miss—"

"Lawson," Gwen supplied, wishing that Stanton Brown hadn't made such a thing of a chance remark. "But I answer to Gwen a lot faster."

"So we're all friends," Lance Fletcher interposed before an awkward silence could develop. "It's a good thing. I'm new at this managering business and it helps to have all the tenants speaking to each other."

Sherry Crane kept her hand on her boss's shoulder but her gaze ran candidly over Lance's tall frame. "I think you could convince most anybody to do things your way, Mr. Fletcher. Isn't that right, Stan?"

"We'll find out," the other man said briskly and got to his feet. "As far as I'm concerned—just keep that sunshine turned on and I'll be happy. Now I'd better get some work done. See you folks later." He shoved his shirt in his trousers before he started back to his villa. It was an automatic gesture and not entirely successful because his girth was considerable. Even his well-tailored slacks and expensive sport shirt couldn't disguise his need to lose at least fifteen pounds.

As Sherry Crane flowed over to pick up a lacy kimono and drape it around her shoulders, it was evident that she didn't have any problems in that sphere. Her figure was pure whistle-bait. In another five years when she reached her early thirties, the adjective might change from voluptuous to full-blown, but at the moment it didn't apply.

Gwen unconsciously let out a wistful sigh and then blushed as she encountered Lance's amused glance. "We have decorative neighbors," she said, keeping her voice light.

"At least one part of the twosome," her aunt confirmed, watching the secretary go toward her villa. "Have you known them long, Lance?"

"About twenty minutes longer than you have. They just arrived yesterday. One of the local real estate men heard about a cancellation on that villa and called me to vouch for Mr. Brown. He didn't mention Miss Crane."

"Not what I'd call a matched pair."

"I'm not so sure." Lance thrust his hands in his pants pockets. "Is it important?"

"Certainly not—it's just nosiness on my part." Pearl got to her feet with an effort. "It comes from living too far out in the country. Cows don't provide very stimulating conversation. Now I think I'll go and lie down a while. It's been a long day already."

"You're all right, aren't you?" Gwen asked anxiously.

"Of course I am." There was a testy note in the older woman's voice. "It was just seeing Miss Crane. She made me feel ten years older suddenly." Her lips twitched as she looked over her shoulder at Lance. "I imagine she triggers that reaction in a lot of people."

He grinned but wasn't to be drawn. "If you need anything, I'll be around later this afternoon."

Pearl smiled and nodded, disappearing slowly into the cottage.

Lance turned back to find a worried look on Gwen's face. "She'll be all right," he said in a surprisingly gentle tone. "This desert sun does do wonders for everybody." He paused for an instant before adding, "Do you think it *was* just plain curiosity about Brown and his secretary?"

"I honestly don't know. They don't ring any bells with me except . . ."

"Except what?" he asked, catching her up quickly.

"Well, Miss Crane could be cloned from a Reno chorus line. A peroxide bottle does have a leveling effect. And I'm *not* being catty. We stopped to see the late show at one of the casinos on the way down here and there were at least four dancers in the front row who looked just like her. The only difference was that they were wearing feather boas instead of a bikini top."

A slow smile creased Lance's tanned face. "I'll bet you were the only one in the audience who remembers the feathers."

"Very probably." Gwen's voice was dry. "If you'd been there, you'd have been concentrating on . . ."

" . . . the clones, I suspect. And whether the feather boas were going to moult in the finale."

"I might have known."

"Exactly." He narrowed his eyes against the sunlight's glare as he continued to stare down at her. "On the other hand, my mind's like a sieve. Can't remember anything from one minute to the next. What did you say your name was?"

"Lawson. *Miss* Lawson. It was at the bottom of the rent check you received last week."

He winced visibly. "Now it comes back to me. I'm new at this business, but I remember that my uncle said never to quarrel with the tenants."

"Where *is* your uncle?"

"Away." Lance gestured vaguely. "He likes to travel."

"Does he always leave you in charge here?"

"Now and then. Whenever he can catch up with me. Or when I run out of money."

"Good Lord! I thought remittance relatives had disappeared with the dodo."

He shook his head solemnly. "There are a few of us still found in southern California, but it's an endangered species."

Gwen wrinkled her nose in disdain. "Well, we'll try not to put you to any trouble while we're here."

"Don't worry, I'll be glad to move pool furniture for you *any* time—" He broke off as her eyes flashed. "Sorry. Maybe we'd better go back to discussing chorus lines—it's safer."

"Why don't you wait for Sherry to come back? Something tells me she's an authority on them. I'm going in to fix a cup of coffee."

"And desert this sunshine? I can recommend the pool." He waved a hand toward the inviting blue water. "I'll even throw in a swimming lesson if that appeals to you."

She raised an eyebrow, annoyed by his implication that anybody who lived north of the Los Angeles city limits would flounder in the shallow end. "I'll struggle along with my inner tube, thanks. You might adjust that umbrella before you go, in case my aunt comes out here again."

"Sure thing." He reached for a dangling chain hanging from the center of the big umbrella. "Which way do you want it?"

"I don't mean the angle," Gwen said and impatiently reached up for a small crank on the other side. "I just meant higher . . ."

"Don't touch *that!*" he commanded, and then ducked as the heavy vinyl umbrella came down around their heads.

Gwen let out a muffled shriek of surprise and scrambled to get out of the way. An instant later, she shrieked again when she found she'd stepped into thin air.

As the pool water closed around her, all she could remember was Lance's amazed expression—tempered more than a little with resigned forebearance.

Chapter Two

When Gwen promptly bobbed back to the surface, her first glance focused on a towering foothill of the San Jacinto mountains, behind the villa, where someone had whitewashed the word "God" on a monumental pile of rocks. There wasn't an exclamation point at the end of it but at that moment she could have supplied one. She heard Lance's voice over the rush of water and rather than face his editorial remarks she simply let herself sink down to the bottom of the pool again.

The next time she surfaced, his strong hand fastened on her upper arm, pulling her to the tile coping. "Look here! Can you swim or can't you?" he wanted to know. "I thought you were kidding about that inner tube, but now I'm not so sure."

She irritably shrugged off his grip. "Of course I can swim. Anyone could tell that!"

"Well, then—what are you hanging around the

bottom for?" He was still eyeing her with some trepidation. "And don't tell me you had a sudden urge to cool off."

"I'm not telling you anything." It was hard for her to maintain any semblance of dignity with water dripping off her nose, her hair in rat tails, and her shirt revealing her measurements with embarrassing accuracy. She become aware of the last as Lance's survey shifted downward and he started to grin. She submerged to chin level again. "Look—just go away, will you! I've done my quota of stupid things for the next six months, so there's no use your hanging around waiting for the next one."

"At least let me help you out of there."

She shook her head, forgetting that the movement would send water spraying. "I can manage. And the way things are going, we'd probably bump heads or I'd get you all wet."

"I'm beginning to believe you. But there's no harm done—unless that wristwatch of yours isn't waterproof."

Gwen looked stricken at his comment and then rallied. "It is, thank heavens. My mind went blank for a moment."

"Probably you're just tired from traveling. I told your aunt that there's always food available over at my place." He jerked his head toward the third villa on the far side of the pool. "All you have to do is let our cook know if you'll be in for meals." He started to leave. "If it's any consolation, I'm not around most of the time so you won't have to worry about colliding with me over a soup dish. You're supposed to enjoy your vacation."

21

"As soon as I can get out of this pool and change my clothes, I'm more apt to," she pointed out.

"I'm leaving right now." He hesitated as if wanting to say more and then obviously changed his mind, disappearing around the corner of the villa.

Once he was out of sight, she didn't waste any time getting out of the pool, giving silent thanks that Stanton Brown and his Sherry hadn't reappeared in the interim.

There was no hiding her appearance from her aunt, however, when she hurried into the villa. "Don't say it," Gwen instructed the older woman who was staring at her dripping figure unbelievingly. "Do you have an extra cup of coffee?"

"Of course. There's plenty." Pearl waved her own cup toward the pot on the stove. "Shall I pour you some now?"

Gwen shook her head and blew her a kiss. "Bless you, no. Let me change first. Otherwise I'll drip on the tile. You know, if this keeps on, I'll run out of clothes before sundown."

Pearl followed her to the bottom of the stair. "Maybe you should follow Miss Crane's example. That way, one suitcase can handle quite a wardrobe." She raised her voice as Gwen started to disappear into the bedroom. "I don't suppose you plan on telling me what happened?"

Her niece's head popped back around the corner of the doorjamb. "Would you believe I wanted a quick dip?"

"Not really. Try again."

Gwen started to unbutton her shirt. "How about our landlord pushing me in?"

"Not on first acquaintance. He isn't the kind to suffer idiotic behavior, but he wouldn't risk that. Which leaves only one alternative."

"Which you knew all along," Gwen mimicked before sneezing abruptly. "You're not helping my ego by rehashing this."

"Not only that—your ego will have a cold in the nose if you don't get out of those clothes," her aunt said austerely. "I'll have your coffee ready when you've changed. And it wouldn't hurt if you held onto the banister when you come back down."

When Gwen appeared in the kitchen a little later, she was wearing a pair of white jeans and a T-shirt that showed a disgruntled knight bearing a broken lance together with the words "Some days the dragon wins."

Her aunt, who was sitting at the round dinette table in the sunlit kitchen, laughed as she read it. "I'm glad that your sense of humor didn't stay at the bottom of the pool. That coffee's just poured. How about a cookie to go with it?"

Gwen pulled out a chair across from her. "No, thanks. Caffeine is all I need just now—not calories. Did you know that there's a catering operation along with this lease? Our landlord mentioned something about meals served at his villa."

Pearl nodded calmly. "Apparently it's a new service and it sounds good to me. I don't know about you, but the thought of avoiding any cooking is marvelous. And it's easier to eat next door than dressing to go out every evening—" She broke off as the telephone sounded from around the corner. "Now what? No, I'll get it," she instructed Gwen, who

23

had started to push back her chair. "Drink your coffee while you have a chance."

Gwen nodded and reached over to turn on a radio which was on the end of the kitchen counter. It took some tuning to find the kind of music she wanted, and after that, she leaned back in her chair, sipping the hot coffee as she stared out onto the deserted patio. It was such a peaceful sunlit vista that she'd almost decided to move back out there when her aunt reentered the room.

Gwen observed her flushed face with interest. "You look as if you'd heard some good news."

"It was Louisa Carlton. They've just arrived to open up their house here."

"That's wonderful! I had no idea that your old chum was coming this month."

Her aunt winced slightly. "You make her sound like Methuselah."

"I didn't mean to," Gwen hurried to say. "Is she coming over?"

Pearl bit her lip. "Actually she's sending Dennis over to fetch us for dinner. I told her that I wasn't sure of your plans, though," she added when Gwen let the silence lengthen. "I swear I didn't know that he was going to be here."

Gwen managed a crooked smile. "I believe you. He's just so darned persistent."

"You must admit he's nice to have around."

"So's a tin of caviar—but you don't want a steady diet of it. His mother should stop signing checks for him."

Pearl sighed and went over to rinse her coffee cup before putting it on the counter. "Probably it's the other way around. Dennis inherited a fair part of his grandfather's ranch."

"Well, it's a good thing he sold it. He only recognizes prime beef on a menu."

"Louisa says he's doing very well in his real estate ventures," Pearl pointed out. "Just because he was born on a ranch doesn't mean he has to spend his life there."

"I know." Gwen grimaced apologetically. "He's nice and I'm being difficult."

"You've had a bad day. He might come in handy as an escort while we're here."

"I hadn't thought of that," Gwen acknowledged. She recalled Lance Fletcher's expression as he'd left her at the pool and decided that it wouldn't hurt to have a presentable male visible on the horizon.

" . . . so how about it?"

Gwen surfaced belatedly. "I beg your pardon?"

"Are you going to accept Louisa's dinner invitation?"

"Not this time." She ran her fingers through her still-damp hair. "I need refurbishing before crossing the Carlton threshold. Dennis prefers women without a hair out of place."

"From what I've heard, he'd take you any way at all."

"You shouldn't believe half of what Louisa reports." Gwen looked at her watch. "When's he coming to collect you?"

"In a half hour." A frown creased Pearl's serene brow. "What will you do for dinner? This might be a good time to try out Mr. Fletcher's cook."

"I've seen all I need of our landlord today without facing him across a dinner table, too. I'll phone and invite Dennis for lunch or something tomorrow." She moved across to drop a kiss on her aunt's cheek. "Have fun and give my best to Louisa."

"How about Dennis?" When Gwen stared, perplexed, Pearl said, "Do I give *him* your best, too?"

"You're too old to start playing Cupid," Gwen said with mock severity. "I'll see you later."

The forecourt of the Desert Villas was deserted as she walked out to her parked car. She could feel the heat of the desert sun seeping through the thin cotton of her T-shirt, and it was a delightful change after a severe northern winter. There was a slight haze in the California sky, though, showing that the Los Angeles smog was barely blocked by the San Jacinto mountains—a problem that Montana residents didn't have to combat.

Gwen didn't waste any time rolling down the car window beside her as she drove off, and even the slightly humid breeze felt wonderful on her face as she finally turned onto East Palm Canyon Drive, heading toward nearby Rancho Mirage and Palm Desert. A supermarket was a supermarket, whatever the suburb.

When she eventually stopped for a red light at an intersection, the man in the car next to her looked enough like Dennis Carlton to make her do a double take before she discovered it was merely a fleeting resemblance. As the light changed, she drove on automatically, but her thoughts were concerned with the Carltons' unexpected appearance at the desert resort. Since she had been deliberately vague about her own arrival date in Palm Springs and hadn't mentioned the Desert Villas at all, she could only presume that Louisa had extracted the information from Pearl. Even that was harmless enough if the widow had been on her own, but Dennis' coming on the scene made it considerably more sticky for Gwen.

She'd known him for some years after he and his mother had arrived to claim his grandfather's estate, but it was only during the past six months that he'd decided to annex Gwen along with his real estate interests. And since she hadn't wanted to cause trouble between the two families, she'd tried to soften her refusals whenever he brought up the subject of marriage. It was like hitting a stone wall. Dennis was convinced that she'd change her mind once she discovered all the advantages to such a merger. His tactical efforts were effective enough that occasionally Gwen wondered why she didn't succumb; he was a handsome escort, their family backgrounds wouldn't conflict, and she knew that both Pearl and Louisa would be pleased with the nuptials.

Dennis was astute enough not to force the issue romantically; his kisses at her front door were pleasant and thorough—letting her feel his desire but quick to break the embrace as soon as Gwen put a hand against his chest. Sometimes she had wished that he wasn't quite such a gentleman, wondering if she'd react differently without that careful lid on his emotions. But such moments were fleeting as her common sense triumphed. The only result of such action would be a definite rift in their friendship—the very thing she'd tried to avoid.

Gwen had to brake suddenly as the car in front of her made an illegal left turn, and she realized there was too much traffic for daydreaming. When the next intersection revealed a modern shopping mall, she turned into it with relief. Anyhow, there was no use going over the same fruitless argument. This time, Dennis would have to be convinced that his studied approach to matrimony wasn't going to work. With Sherry Crane in the immediate neighborhood the decision might not be too painful for him. Lance Fletcher had certainly been enjoying the scenery at the poolside earlier in the day.

That momentary memory made Gwen miss a break in the traffic as she waited to pull into the parking lot. An impatient honking from the car behind her brought her back to earth in a hurry and she didn't waste any time then, accelerating to find an empty place.

There were some attractive stores around the mall and she took her time windowshopping at the various boutiques which surrounded the supermarket. An especially attractive hairdressing salon nearby made her pause as she surveyed her reflection in the display window. Following an impulse, she went into the shop and was lucky enough to get a cancellation. It was all very well to have a short haircut which behaved creditably well, but feminine instinct convinced Gwen that it wasn't good enough.

She submitted happily to the ministrations of a good stylist who snipped some stray ends and suggested a new way of brushing back the sides so that her hair looked like a gleaming cap.

"Only somebody with bone structure like yours could get away with the style," the operator said finally. "And the great part is, it falls into place without any special setting. Just right for Palm Springs, where you're in and out of a swimming pool all day."

"That's certainly the truth," Gwen confirmed wryly. She checked her appearance in the mirror and nodded. "I like it. It's comfortable and . . ."

" . . . very feminine," the other finished for her. "Just a few minutes under the dryer is all you'll need now."

Gwen was following the stylist toward the row of dryers at the rear of the salon when a familiar figure straightened nearby.

"Well, what do you know—it's my new neighbor," Sherry Crane murmured in dulcet tones. "You find your way around the town fast, Gwen honey. If I'd known you were coming here, I could have hitched a ride instead of having to bother Lance."

"You mean he's here?" Startled, Gwen turned toward the front of the salon.

"Not now." Sherry was taking in Gwen's jeans and T-shirt with a slight smile. "But you don't have to worry—informality is the thing in Palm Springs. That's one reason Stan and I like it so much." As she spoke, she smoothed the waistband of her white gabardine slacks, unconsciously calling attention to the fact that there wasn't a pound out of place in that vicinity. It wasn't difficult to ascertain, since the slacks clung like a second skin. The jersey halter Sherry wore atop them covered more territory than the bikini bra she'd worn at the pool, but the fabric was still minimal. Sherry's measurements weren't, and she was hard to ignore.

"You've come to the right place," she went on,

eyeing Gwen's hairdo. "That style does something for you."

"Thank you." Gwen caught sight of the operator who was still waiting for her at the dryer. "I'll have to go. If you want a ride back, I'll not be long. I just have some grocery shopping . . ." Her voice trailed off as Sherry smiled and shook her head.

"Thanks—but Lance is on his way. Normally I have a driver, but Stan needed the car this afternoon." She smiled slowly, the movement almost feline. "Lance didn't seem to mind at all, though. He's sweet, isn't he?"

Gwen managed a noncommittal nod, even as she glanced warily toward the front of the shop again.

"You'll have to get better acquainted," Sherry said, patting her arm as if to console her. "Are you going to join us for dinner at his place tonight? Lance says that he has a fabulous cook."

"So I heard." Gwen tried to make her tone regretful. "I'm sorry that I can't make it. The Carltons—they're neighbors from Montana—have just arrived in town and invited us for the evening." She saw no need to explain that she had no intention of joining either gathering.

"Well, there's lots of time. We can all get together some other night," Sherry said, not sounding heartbroken over the way things turned out either. She did bestow a thoughtful look on Gwen before waggling red-tipped fingers in a graceful farewell. Then she undulated—there was no other word for it—to the front of the shop and out the door.

A little later, when Gwen was finished, she emerged more cautiously from the beauty salon. It only took a hasty look at the rows of parked cars to reveal that Lance had already picked up his package. Not that there was any shortage of attractive blondes in the nearby supermarket; she discovered that as she started her grocery shopping. Apparently glamour pervaded every facet of life at the resort—making her doubly glad that she'd taken time to improve her own appearance.

The early evening shadows were giving the San Jacinto mountains a striking blue-purple cast as Gwen drove back to the villa a little later. When the sun finally dropped behind the mountain range, the temperature dropped as well, but the air was still in the "balmy" category. Even the traffic congestion had eased, allowing her to relax and note the many eating places along the roadside. For an instant, she wondered if she was silly to choose a solitary television dinner on her first night at the resort, and then her chin firmed. It wasn't a question of "choosing," exactly; "retreating" was a more accurate term. But just then it was more appealing than coping with the Carltons or Lance Fletcher and Sherry.

As Gwen pulled up in the curving drive to park in front of her villa, the palms edging the well-manicured lawn were casting giant shadows. The faint gold bands of sunlight remaining on the side of the villa could have been daubed on by a French impressionist, but a closer glimpse showed that it was merely the texture of the stucco which created the interesting effect. Gwen balanced a bag of groceries on one hip as she unlocked the door and, once inside, called out "Aunt Pearl?"

There was only an answering silence, confirming

that her aunt hadn't changed her plans for the evening. Gwen pushed the door shut behind her and made her way to the deserted kitchen.

It was when she was unpacking the groceries and stowing frozen dinners in the freezer that she heard a sudden sound from the living room. She stood motionless—waiting to see if the sound was repeated. When nothing more happened, she frowned and closed the refrigerator before going around the corner to the television alcove. Her frown deepened as she tried to decide if she'd been imagining things. A sudden impulse made her go over and peer out the door onto the patio. That proved a total loss because both the patio and the pool were unoccupied.

She walked out onto the patio then and stared toward the villa which Stanton Brown and Sherry were renting. Draperies covered the windows facing the pool, suggesting that the tenants were either having dinner with their landlord or enjoying privacy at home.

Gwen shook her head and walked back into her own house. She hovered uncertainly before making a systematic search of the premises.

A few minutes later, she was back in the kitchen turning on the oven and trying to forget her momentary spell of the jitters. Strange houses make strange noises, she'd decided, but that logical conclusion didn't keep her from sliding the extra bolt on the front door when she'd put her dinner in the oven. After that, she went up to change into a cotton robe for lounging in front of the television as she ate. She frowned as she opened a bureau drawer to extract a handkerchief, thinking that she'd been untidier than she realized when she'd unpacked. That was consistent with her behavior during the rest of the day, she decided. The only thing left was to burn her frozen dinner, and she glanced at her watch to make sure *that* wasn't a possibility.

The rest of the evening passed uneventfully. While dinner wasn't a gourmet delight, it wasn't bad. Just about the same rating she gave to the television movie she watched later. During one of the commercial intermissions, she thought she heard voices by the poolside but resolutely resisted an impulse to peer through the draperies and confirm it.

It wasn't any of her affair whether Sherry Crane and her Mr. Brown were just then returning from dinner with Lance. Gwen stayed firmly ensconced in her corner of the davenport with her attention on the screen until the voices outside subsided to a murmur and then disappeared altogether.

When the movie finally ended, she stood up to switch off the set. A glance at her watch made her frown thoughtfully. Normally her aunt would have returned from a dinner engagement long before. It was especially puzzling since Pearl was recuperating and had agreed to get plenty of sleep on the holiday.

Gwen yawned and decided that she was being overly concerned. Her aunt was a sensible person and certainly old enough to make her own decisions. Probably she'd gotten immersed in talking to Louisa and hadn't kept track of the time.

Detouring by the kitchen for a glass of milk, Gwen climbed the stairs a few minutes later and got ready for bed. She turned off the airconditioner and opened a window, taking a breath of cool night air before going back to her comfortable mattress. It felt wonderful to stretch out between the smooth, fresh-smelling sheets. She'd have to give Lance Fletcher full marks for the housekeeping at the Desert Villas. Either the man was lucky in hiring staff or he doubled as an upstairs maid whenever new tenants were in the offing. Gwen smiled at that thought and then yawned hugely as she reached over to turn off the lamp by her bed.

She'd bet her bottom dollar that cleaning a swimming pool was the only domestic task that Lance undertook. That, together with endorsing a monthly check from his uncle and welcoming blondes to the dinner table, probably exhausted the man's strength.

Not that it mattered, Gwen told herself sleepily, because she didn't intend to have any more to do with their landlord than she could help.

It was on that fervent but not very unique decision that her eyelids went down and stayed that way.

Chapter Three

Considerably later, Gwen's slumber was interrupted by a none-too-gentle shaking. She opened her eyes and blinked, owl-like, in the bright light flooding the room. It took an instant longer to focus on the figure bending over her bed. Then she shot to a sitting position, gasping, "What are you doing here?"

Lance, seeing the alarm in her face, promptly put a large hand over her mouth to stifle the scream which was in the making. "Pipe down, will you! There's no need to raise the whole neighborhood. Believe me, this isn't my idea." He saw her eyebrows come together in a scowl as his words registered, but pressed on, "I haven't ravished anybody in the last day or two so you can relax. Actually I'm just here to deliver a message—" Gwen mumbled something, but it was in a low tone so he lowered his hand. "Your aunt called."

As Gwen's initial alarm subsided, another rose to

take its place. She hastily rebuttoned her thin pajama top which had come adrift during her sleep. "Why on earth did she call you? Pearl's all right, isn't she?"

Lance shoved her feet aside and sat down on the edge of the mattress. "I've been bending over you so long that the blood's gone to my head," he complained. "Of course she's all right. Don't you ever let anybody get a word in edgeways?"

His brusqueness reassured her more effectively than he knew. Gwen took time to push back from his tall figure and pull the sheet up to her chin, but she said calmly, "It's a good thing you didn't go in for medicine. You have a terrible bedside manner."

Lance scowled across at her. "There haven't been any complaints about it till now. Do you want to hear what I've come to say or don't you?"

Her chin went up. "That's the only reason you're still sitting there, believe me."

His glance raked her coldly. "I'm glad that we agree on something. Your aunt's been trying to reach you ever since midnight to say that she's spending the night with her friends. When she couldn't get any answer, she started to worry." He looked pointedly at the bedside table. "Most tenants move the phone up here at night. You can't hear it ringing from downstairs."

"I'm sorry—I wasn't expecting any calls." Belatedly she realized that he was wearing a blue pajama top and had apparently pulled a pair of cotton slacks over the bottoms in his haste to reach her. She shifted against the headboard, adding defensively, "You could have just knocked on the door."

He smacked his forehead with the palm of his

hand. "My God, I've been beating on it for the better part of ten minutes. If I hadn't seen your car outside, I would have sworn you weren't home. I was ready to call in the paramedics—then I decided to check with a passkey first."

Probably he expected to find an empty gin bottle or pill container by the edge of her pillow, Gwen thought. A gurgle of laughter rose in her throat and she kept her tone level with an effort. "I'm sorry," she managed, "I must have been more tired than I thought." She knew it was a lame excuse, but it happened to be the truth.

He was still eyeing her suspiciously. "Your aunt mentioned that you were a deep sleeper or I'd have been even more alarmed."

Color rose in her cheeks. There was nothing like a discussion of intimate habits to put things on an informal basis, she thought irritably. It wasn't like Pearl to be so forthcoming with a comparative stranger. "I'm surprised she didn't call earlier. I was in all evening."

His eyebrows went up. "I thought you were invited out to dinner. Sherry said something about it." When Gwen stirred uncomfortably under his gaze but didn't offer any explanation, he went on, "Anyhow, your aunt planned to come back tonight but she—had a little difficulty."

"What does that mean?" Gwen asked, feeling the first shaft of fear. "I thought you said she was all right."

"She is. It was the fellow driving who took the worst of it. Dennis somebody or other."

Gwen forgot all about her clutch on the sheet as

she sat straight up. "Carlton. Look, tell me what happened, will you? I wish you'd stop tippy-toeing around."

"It was a traffic collision of sorts," Lance said in a flat tone. "Apparently this Dennis was run off the road and whacked his head when he hit the side window in the process. Your aunt was wearing her seat belt so she was just shaken up a bit. Scout's honor," Lance professed, raising his hand, "that's what she said."

Gwen made a dive toward the foot of the bed for her robe. "Well, I want to call her. Is she at a hospital?"

"Nope. She's back home with her friend Louisa. Dennis was released too—once they'd checked him over in the Emergency Room.

Gwen was tying the belt on her cotton robe and sliding into a pair of scuffs at the same time. "I can't understand why Aunt Pearl didn't come on home."

"Because Louisa was all shook up about what happened. Apparently she wanted somebody to hold her hand."

"I suppose she was upset because her son was hurt—" Gwen was starting toward the bedroom door when she pulled up. "Golly, I don't know their number, and I'll bet it's unlisted."

Lance got to his feet and fished in the pocket of his pajama top, finally pulling out a scrap of paper. "Here it is. Your aunt thought you'd need it tomorrow morning. That's when she's expecting your call."

Gwen took the paper from him, and stood uncertainly in the doorway. "Is that what she said?"

He nodded reassuringly. "And she wanted to tell you that she'll be back after breakfast." When Gwen still hesitated, he said, "As long as we're both wide-awake, we might as well have something hot to drink. You can decide then what you want to do. Is there anything in your refrigerator or would you rather come to my place?"

"That isn't necessary." She started for the stairs with him at her heels. "There's milk for cocoa—if that sounds good. Or I can make coffee."

"Any cookies?" He followed her into the kitchen and looked around hopefully.

Her lips quirked upward as she stopped in front of the refrigerator. "In that top drawer."

"Good. Then instant coffee will do."

"You're not worried about staying awake?"

He lounged against the corner of the breakfast table and watched her fill the teakettle. "Insomnia's not a problem of mine. As a matter of fact, your aunt had to ring for quite a while before she roused me."

His confession unaccountably made Gwen feel better. She flashed him a shy smile over her shoulder as she reached in the cupboard for two mugs, having decided to follow his lead and try some coffee. She was so wide-awake by then that even caffeine couldn't do any more damage.

By the time the water boiled, she'd arranged cookies on a plate and put instant coffee in the mugs. Lance waved her aside as he turned off the teakettle and filled the mugs, bringing them over to the table afterwards. He waited for her to sit down and then pulled out a chair beside her. "I don't know whether this counts as afterdinner coffee or predawn breakfast." He picked up the steaming mug. "Anyhow, cheers!"

She nodded and took a careful sip. "Help yourself to the cookies. I hope you like chocolate chip."

"One of my favorites." He reached out a tanned hand. "Chen usually bakes them once a week." Seeing Gwen's puzzled expression, he added, "Chen's the cook and general factotum. You'd have met him if you'd come to dinner."

She murmured something about being sorry she'd missed out and took refuge in another swallow of coffee. That time, she forgot how hot it was and winced as it went down. "You didn't say whether anybody else was hurt when Dennis' car ran off the road tonight," she said, managing to change the subject. "Was the other driver injured?"

"Your aunt didn't say. I suppose she would have mentioned it if there was anything serious. My guess is that it was some hotrodder who decided the whole highway was his."

Gwen nodded solemnly. "You're probably right. I'm thankful that it wasn't worse. The last thing my aunt needs right now is another hospital stay."

"She told me she was recuperating from surgery. Don't worry—she didn't sound as if tonight's experience had set her back." Lance looked sympathetically at her over the top of his mug and Gwen wondered suddenly how she could ever have thought that his face was forbidding. His next words, though, showed that his thinking hadn't mellowed to the same extent. "You'd better get back up to bed, or you'll be dragging tomorrow. And don't worry about this," he gestured toward the clutter on the table. "I'll clean it up before I leave. *And* lock the door behind me." He frowned as he peered across at her. "You are all right, aren't you?"

"I'm fine," she snapped, wishing that he'd stop sounding like a camp counselor. "It's just been an ..."

" ... unnerving experience," he finished for her. "I know and I'm sorry. But your aunt and I thought you'd want to know."

"Well, naturally. I'll probably see you tomorrow," she said, getting to her feet.

"No doubt about it. And if you can't face cooking breakfast, Chen is always around."

No wonder he looked so complacent, she thought. A jewel of a cook safely tucked away and apparently no shortage of takers for his hospitality. "I'll keep it in mind."

Apparently he didn't linger long in tidying the kitchen because Gwen heard the door close shortly after she went upstairs. By then, she'd shed her robe and was staring grimly at her tousled reflection in the mirror above the dressing table. No wonder Lance hadn't lost any time sending her on her way!

She went over to get into bed, making sure that she hadn't misplaced the telephone number for the Carltons' Palm Springs house. Just then, she could have used some of Pearl's unflappable common sense. She could only hope that she'd be on her way back home early in the morning.

But when her aunt did reappear shortly after breakfast, Gwen found that she wasn't going to be able to count on the older woman's presence as she'd thought.

Once Pearl had reassured her that she was feeling fine and only had a bruised elbow as a memento of the occasion, she lost no time in announcing her newest plans. "Gwen dear, if you don't mind—Louisa has asked me to spend this week with her in Phoenix. Dennis was going along to help with the driving, but he's out of the picture now."

"Why? He's not badly hurt, is he?" Gwen asked, ignoring the first announcement in light of the other news.

"His pride took the worst of it. Even so, Louisa wouldn't leave him except that she has to sign the closing papers on the sale of some of their Arizona property. Dennis has assured her that he'll be perfectly all right."

"I *did* wonder when you appeared in that taxi this morning. You should have called me."

"There was no need. Dennis' car is still being repaired and Louisa hadn't received her rental for the Phoenix trip, so they insisted on sending me back in a taxi." Her aunt sighed humorously. "You know how adamant they both can be."

"That's putting it mildly."

"You don't mind, do you? My going away, I mean? I know that you said you needed company on your vacation, but I had the feeling you were just making sure that I found some sunshine after that hospital. And now I'm planning to leave you here alone." Pearl held out her palms in mock dismay. "I'm an ungrateful old woman."

Gwen grinned and gave her a hug. "You're the nicest relative I have."

"I'll ignore the fact that I'm practically the only one," Pearl responded, as she returned the hug and then held the younger woman at arm's length. "I won't be gone long. There's a condominium that Louisa wants me to see in Phoenix, too."

"Well, take a good look. There's nothing nicer than having an aunt who owns an apartment in the sun belt," Gwen assured her.

Pearl arched her eyebrows. "Good heavens, anybody would think you couldn't afford one yourself! Dennis believes you're foolish to spend so much of your life at the ranch."

"I wish he'd stop proclaiming it like the town crier." Gwen went over to sit on the edge of the bed, watching her aunt pack her small suitcase. "He never stops mentioning money—and I don't think he'll ever get enough of it. Even when he's ninety." She sighed and leaned back on her palms. "How will he like having to suffer in solitude? Or is he going to try and track down that driver who ran you off the road?"

"There's small chance of that since it was so dark. Dennis was bringing me back here and suddenly there was this long car right beside us. In fairness to Dennis, he didn't have any choice. Fortunately, there was some shoulder to the highway along there. If we'd been up in a canyon—" Pearl broke off, shuddering.

Gwen nodded, her own expression grim. "But couldn't the police be looking for a damaged car?"

"Dennis didn't report it to the police, so far as I know."

"For heaven's sake, why not?"

"Because we couldn't get the license number or identify the make of car. And it wasn't damaged because there wasn't any collision. All our bruises came when Dennis went off the road and slammed on the brakes."

"Well, it doesn't seem fair . . ."

"There's an old saying about 'Not bothering to shoe the goose.' Why should we waste our time?" Pearl shook her head and then resumed her packing. "Just be grateful that no one was seriously hurt."

"Dennis will miss having somebody hold his hand. He's used to lots of creature comforts."

Pearl was closing her case but she looked up to say thoughtfully, "I'd guess he plans to recuperate with you by his side."

"Oh, help!"

"I *did* tell him you had quite a round of things planned."

"I don't—but I'm sure as heck going to find some. If he wants mothering, he'd better follow Louisa and you to Phoenix." Gwen got to her feet as a knock sounded on the front door. "That must be your cabdriver. I'll go tell him you're nearly ready. Let me have your case."

"It isn't heavy . . ."

"Too heavy for *you*, so don't argue." Gwen took it from her and started for the stairs. "Don't forget a topcoat. You might need it if the weather turns. And call me when you know where you're staying."

"Yes, dear." Her aunt's amused voice followed her down the stairs. "And you accuse *me* of fussing."

The cab, with Pearl waving from the back seat, was pulling out of the drive a little later when Lance came around the corner of the villa. His sudden appearance gave Gwen a start as she turned to go back in the house.

"I didn't see you," she said, trying to hide her confusion. "You just missed saying good-bye to my aunt."

"Good-bye?" His dark brows drew together. "What happened? I thought she was planning to stay here a while."

"Palm Springs is losing out to Phoenix for the time being." Gwen lingered on the front steps and, as he didn't show any indication of moving on, gestured inside. "There's coffee—if you'd like some."

"Thanks, but I've already had mine." His words stopped for an instant as he bestowed a thoughtful, searching glance. "On the other hand, another cup of coffee might do the trick. I'm moving slower than usual this morning." He waved her ahead of him and closed the door before following her to the kitchen. "This looks familiar."

"I can't understand why. Go ahead and sit down. I'll just dump these in the sink for the moment," she said, whisking away some dirty dishes and getting out a clean cup and saucer. "There are some hot cinnamon rolls in the oven."

"No, thanks." He was watching her move around the kitchen and seemed to approve of what he saw. "It's too bad that you weren't included in the jaunt to Arizona."

"I don't mind a bit," Gwen said truthfully. "She's going with a friend, so that lets me keep the home fires burning. Not literally," she added with a smile as she poured coffee and put it in front of him. "You don't have to worry."

"I wasn't." His grin was slow. "There's a hefty damage clause included in that lease you signed for your aunt."

Gwen started to say that her aunt didn't have anything to do with the transaction and then thought better of it. "It's standard practice," she finished weakly, meeting his glance.

"Well, don't worry about it. Neither of you looks like the home-wrecking type. Of course, you *are* a little hard on sun umbrellas . . ."

"I thought we were going to forget about that. As well as some other things." She stood with the coffeepot poised purposefully.

"My mind just went blank," he said, hurriedly. But when she nodded and topped her own coffee cup, he probed further. "Does this mean that you'll be flopping around with nothing to do? While your aunt's gone?"

She stared at him, not exactly sure what he meant. "Well, I won't be acting as chauffeur or cook for a few days."

"How about taking on a part-time job to make a little extra money? Your aunt couldn't object if it didn't interfere with your regular duties for her." When Gwen's lips parted in amazement, he leaned forward on the table to emphasize his point. "Actually I could use some help. I'm sort of in a mess."

She surveyed his intent figure with a puzzled look.

He was dressed casually in jeans and a plaid cotton shirt but his tanned skin exuded a faint aroma of citrus shaving lotion and his dark hair was still damp from a shower or early dip. Aside from the wrinkles at the corners of his eyes, which could have been caused by a lack of sleep, his new problems hadn't affected him visibly. Therefore her voice was wary as she asked, "Exactly what kind of a mess?"

"Not drug-running or white slavery, if that's what's on your mind. You've watched too many television movies."

"I don't deny it." Her expression eased at his words but she didn't relax. "It's been a long winter at home and our neighbors aren't within shouting distance."

"Well, if you help me out, I can guarantee to enlarge your social acquaintance. My cook wants to take a few days off."

"The fabulous Chen?" Gwen started to smile. "What's so tragic about that? You can begin defrosting television dinners like the rest of us."

"Maybe *I* could, but I doubt if Sherry and her chum Stanton would go for it. Part of the lease stipulates that we have meals available. They could sue, if worst came to worst." He looked down at his coffee and swirled it absently. "As a matter of fact, so could you. Or at least, break the lease."

"I see." Her tone was chastened. "That could be expensive for you?"

"Very expensive. This place doesn't come cheap in season."

"I remember." She thought for a moment and then

said, "All you have to do is call an agency that handles temporary help."

He shook his head slowly. "So speaks the innocent. Getting the right kind of temporary employee at this time of year is out of the question. Security in Palm Springs is as important as experience. I wouldn't have to worry about that if you'd help me out."

"I might be long on security, but I'm pretty short on experience."

His eyebrows shot up. "Don't people in Montana cook for ranch hands and harvesters?"

"I'm not the only one who's been watching too many television movies," she informed him tartly. "Montana's a big state and the natives come in all shapes and sizes." It was a temptation to announce that she employed a very good cook for the ranch who was taking a well-deserved vacation just then.

Lance must have thought that her hesitation meant only that she needed a little more persuading because he said, "Pearl told me that you'd handled all her business affairs while she was in the hospital. Working in the kitchen won't be any harder. I can help you out and the extra money won't be a detriment."

It was all coming too fast for Gwen. Only one word registered in that lot. "Money," she said dazedly.

"Well, of course. I wouldn't expect you to do it out of the goodness of your heart. If you felt like it, you could even tour Sherry around. She wants to learn more about this area and Stanton isn't cooperating. Naturally, I'd reimburse you for the extra time."

"Naturally." Gwen tried to hide the fact that her brain was seething. Apparently Lance had decided to do her a good turn by lining her pockets with extra cash while Pearl was out of town. What he didn't know was that all the advantages weren't on his side; it would give her a built-in excuse to avoid any plans Dennis might have to hold a sit-in on her patio while he recuperated.

"I didn't think it would take you this long to make up your mind."

She looked up to encounter Lance's brooding gaze and hastily tried to cloak her indecision. "You mentioned taking Miss Crane . . ."

"Call her Sherry—it makes her happier."

"Whatever you say. If I take Sherry around the neighborhood," she said, emphasizing the name wryly, "it's going to be a thin tour. I'm a stranger here myself."

"You can read a map, can't you? Obviously you can," he went on, without giving her a chance to answer. "You found your way to California, so why the big fuss about a little local sightseeing? Actually there's not that much to see—no matter what the Chamber of Commerce claims. Besides, I suspect that Sherry will be hard to dislodge from the side of the swimming pool after one or two excursions." He shoved his empty coffee cup toward the center of the table. "What do you say?"

"Well, if you're sure . . ."

His eyebrows drew together. "I didn't believe you'd be the dithering type. Yes or no?"

She swallowed and crossed her fingers under the table. "Yes."

An expression of relief swept over his face, but it was gone so soon that Gwen wondered if she'd just imagined it. "When do you want me to start?" she asked as he got to his feet. "Right away?"

For the first time, he looked taken aback. "That's not necessary. Chen's not leaving until noon."

"What about lunch? Do Sherry and her chum appear for it?"

"Not at my house. They're strictly on their own until dinner. As a matter of fact, Stan said something about a business conference today."

"That still leaves Sherry on her own," Gwen observed.

He shook his head. "You've put her in the wrong niche. Despite her appearance, she sure sounds like a bona fide secretary."

"You could have fooled me."

He grinned at her feline response. "That will teach you to go strictly by first impressions. It's a good thing I didn't make the same mistake with you."

He left shortly after that—before Gwen could ask exactly what he meant. She cast a wry look down at her pink wraparound skirt which she'd paired with a whimsical pink elephant print blouse. It certainly wasn't reflecting her mood just then—so perhaps Lance had a point.

She didn't waste any time straightening the kitchen, having a strong premonition that Dennis would soon be making an appearance. When the front doorbell gave its muted summons, Gwen checked the time as she went to answer it.

"It's eleven-thirty," she said, not at all surprised

to find his tall figure on the doorstep. "Just in time for lunch."

"That's not a very enthusiastic way to say hello," he said, taking off his sunglasses to reveal a bruised forehead and a partially-blackened eye.

Compassion swept over Gwen and she drew him inside. "I'm sorry. Aunt Pearl told me what a miserable time you had. At least you're vertical today, and that's something to be thankful for."

"You wouldn't be such a Pollyanna if you had my headache," he told her, allowing himself to be led into the television alcove where he collapsed on the couch and closed his eyes. "I hope you have an ice bag."

"I'll look around." Gwen stood looking down at him. Even with his discolored skin, his profile was impressive, and one piece of his thick fair hair fell over his broad forehead, making him look more vulnerable than usual. She'd learned weeks ago that his youthful air was deceptive, that his blue eyes could be remarkably appraising when the occasion demanded—revealing every one of his twenty-nine years. Taking the weather into consideration, he'd worn a white linen blazer which provided a nice contrast to his blue gabardine slacks and sports shirt. He wasn't unaware of his appearance, Gwen knew, and she watched him shift surreptitiously to avoid wrinkling the back of his jacket.

When the silence lengthened between them, his eyelids rose and he stared up accusingly at her. "What gives?"

She smiled. "I was just thinking that you're the only man I know who makes a black eye look good.

How did you ever avoid modeling shirts on television?"

He snorted, but his tone was much more amiable when he replied, "Flattery might get you an invitation to lunch, but I need that ice bag first. They told me at the hospital to use one if I wanted to keep the swelling down."

"Are you sure you should be up at all?"

"Oh, for God's sake, Gwen—you sound like my mother, and I had a hard enough time getting her out of town. Why do you think I'm so late?"

"I didn't know you were coming at all," Gwen said, not quite truthfully. "Sit still—I'll find the ice bag. I think I saw one upstairs in the linen closet."

When she came down again, ice bag in hand, he got stiffly to his feet. "I didn't mean to sound off. Once I swallow another cup of coffee and some aspirin, I'll be all set to take you out to lunch."

Gwen almost offered to fix him something at the villa but decided that might come under the category of "fussing" as well. "I'll have to change," she said while getting ice cubes from the freezer and filling the bag. She saw him go over and test the coffeepot on the counter. "Sorry, there's nothing left, but it won't take long to make you some."

"Instant will do." He took the ice bag from her and headed back toward the other room.

The combination of ice, coffee, and aspirin apparently had its desired effect, because when Gwen came down the stairs a little later, dressed in a blue and white seersucker suit with a crisp white pique blouse, Dennis was able to flash a smile as he got to his feet.

"That's my girl. You look lovely! A little pale, maybe, but the desert sun should take care of that."

"I meant to ask how you stay so tanned. All we got at home this winter was snow blindness. You must have cheated." She was transferring her wallet to a straw purse as she spoke.

"Not at all. I spent a few days skiing in Colorado not long ago. Didn't you miss me?"

He spoke with the assurance of a man whom very few women had forgotten, once they'd managed an introduction.

Gwen saw no harm in jarring his complacency a little bit. "Between visiting Aunt Pearl in the hospital every day and driving all that way home again, I was going steady with my car radio. There wasn't time for anything else."

"Sweetie, I'm sorry. It slipped my mind."

"Considering the beating you've taken in the last twenty-four hours, I'm not surprised. Anyhow"—she tucked the purse under her arm and opened the door—"everything had a happy ending. I hope you've brought plenty of money for lunch. I'm starved!"

The sight of a strange car parked in front of the villa made Gwen's steps slow for a moment until she recalled that her aunt had mentioned that Dennis' car was being repaired. "The rental car company must be enjoying the extra business from the Carlton family. This *is* a rental, isn't it?"

He pulled open the door of the modest sedan with more force than absolutely necessary. "You've never seen me driving anything like it before, have you?"

"Well, it won't be forever," she said, trying to placate him after he'd handed her in and gone around to slide behind the steering wheel. "So long as it has four wheels and goes, it doesn't matter."

He gave her an austere look before starting the engine and pulling out into the drive. "Not all of us feel the same way. A car like this doesn't have any soul."

"But sports cars do? I must remember that." She noted that he turned down the highway toward Palm Desert and Rancho Mirage rather than heading back to Palm Springs. "Are we going anyplace special?"

"There's a tolerable restaurant not too far away." He accelerated into the fast lane of traffic before favoring her with a sidelong glance. "Unless you'd rather take advantage of the chaperones leaving town."

She pretended to consult her watch. "It's so early for an orgy. You can't mean that there's a catch to our lunch date?"

"I wish you'd take me seriously now and then."

"I thought that's the last thing a man wanted a woman to do."

"Very funny." He braked forcefully as a traffic light turned red and shifted in the seat to face her. "How would you like a trip to Las Vegas? The sun shines on swimming pools there just as well as at Palm Springs."

"So I've heard." She stared back at him, puzzled. "Are you talking about an afternoon excursion?"

"Do I look like the type to take a tour?" He went on persuasively, without waiting for an answer. "I was thinking about spending a few days there. We could try our luck at the tables and take in the shows on the strip." When a horn blared behind them, he swore under his breath and turned back to his driving. "We might as well be in Las Vegas as here. Well, what do you say?"

"It's the nicest invitation I've had today—" she began, only to have him cut in impatiently.

"That phrase usually comes before 'but.' What's the matter? Are you afraid of what Pearl might think?"

"I don't need written permission, if that's what you mean." She kept her tone light. "But I can't take any time off right now. I have a job."

He swerved into a left-turn lane and waited for a break in the traffic before heading down another busy thoroughfare. "Okay, I'll bite. What kind of a job?"

"Cooking."

He did shoot her an incredulous glance then. "You're kidding!"

Gwen's lips twitched. "It's a good thing my employer didn't hear that."

"You're serious? Who in the hell hired you?"

"Lance Fletcher."

"Who's he?"

"I forgot that you hadn't met. He's the caretaker where we're staying. Actually, I guess he's the manager. His uncle is the one who owns the place, but he's away."

Dennis was so intent on her words that he almost missed turning into the drive of a large Spanish-style building of white stucco with a red-tiled roof. Beds of white petunias provided a mass of bloom beneath towering palms in the landscaping at the front.

"What a pretty place!" Gwen enthused as Dennis

braked under an arched entryway. "I've never seen such flowers!"

"Don't think you're going to get away with changing the subject," Dennis told her grimly, opening his door. "We're just postponing it—although I don't know why. This way, you can spoil my lunch, too."

The color in Gwen's cheeks deepened as she realized the parking attendant who was hovering hadn't missed a word. She took a deep breath and managed to get out of the car without showing how annoyed she was. At times, Dennis displayed an almost Victorian disregard for domestic staff workers, generally ignoring them completely.

Fortunately, their lunch reservation was in order and his manner improved as a maître 'd led them to a table which overlooked a graceful fountain in the flower-filled patio.

As soon as he'd put menus in their hands and disappeared, Gwen took a look around, appreciating the beamed ceiling of the big room, the massive oak buffet beside their table, and the dull red of the quarry tile floor.

There was a peace and serenity about the place which even the busy black-clad waiters and the well-filled tables couldn't disturb. Gwen sneaked a look at Dennis' expression over the top of her menu and hoped for the best.

A few minutes later, after consulting with an elderly waiter, they ordered a house specialty of chicken sautéed in lemon sauce and a fruit salad topped with avocado. The waiter took their menus and left, assuring them that he'd bring the salad right away. Dennis watched him go, then he pushed his sunglasses more firmly on the bridge of his nose and said, "All right, let's have the rest of it."

"There isn't any more. I told Lance—Mr. Fletcher—that I'd help him out for a few days."

Dennis hadn't missed her hesitation over the name. His jaw set even more firmly. "You agreed to a fool idea like that, knowing I was in town?"

"That isn't fair, Dennis." She put up her palms helplessly. "There's nothing—binding—between us."

"Whose fault is that?" He captured her hands and held them secure in his, atop the table. "Gwen, love—don't let's argue. We can charter a plane to Vegas and get married this afternoon. After that, we'll call the dowagers in Phoenix and then take the phone off the hook. What do you say?"

Vainly she tried to escape his clasp. "I wish you wouldn't be so—persistent. You know that it's a lost cause. I've told you before. I don't want to get married."

"All right, then. Let's just go away for the weekend together. Who knows? After a few days you might change your mind about a marriage license." He leaned toward her, tightening his possessive clasp on her hands. "Maybe that's the sensible way to approach things. After all, you aren't exactly immune to me. Oh, hell." The last came as the waiter arrived to serve their salad.

Gwen drew back with relief, thankful for the respite. When the man withdrew, she picked up her fork, and said mildly, "Of course I'm not immune. No woman objects to being kissed. You go about it very nicely."

"Only because I wanted to impress you." Dennis stared down at his salad as if it offended him. "I knew better than to try and rush things. That's all right for some women but—"

"—not for the long term?" she finished dryly. "Well, you can't claim to be the perfect gentleman. One of those wouldn't be discussing his technique." She took another bite of avocado. "At least I'm learning what makes you tick."

He drew back, obviously nettled, to pick up his own fork and attack his salad. "I'm glad that I'm good for something as far as you're concerned."

Gwen started to utter some soothing comment but changed her mind, concentrating on the food in front of her instead. She'd learned from experience that once Dennis settled into a "doom and gloom" mood, he was hard to jolly out of it. In this case, it would take too drastic measures. She had no intention of going to Las Vegas with him—either with a marriage license providing the lure or without.

At least he wasn't apt to try any strong-arm methods once they got back in the car. His approach to lovemaking was so brisk that it was almost calculated. For a man whose outward appearance fairly oozed male sensuality, his actual emotions seemed barely skin-deep.

Nevertheless, she decided, it wouldn't hurt to try and change the subject.

Dennis looked up then and beat her to it. "This landlord of yours. How old is he?"

She started to laugh helplessly, saying finally, "I don't know what it has to do with anything, but he's older than you."

"How much older?" Dennis persisted stubbornly.

"Four or five years, I guess. Somewhere in his early thirties. I don't know the man well enough to ask him. Why in the world do you care?"

"I wondered what prompted you to take the job, if you must know. Does he think you're doing it for the money?"

Gwen could feel heat stealing up her face and hoped that it wasn't too noticeable. She kept her attention firmly on the salad in front of her as she protested, "Honestly, I don't know why you're asking all these questions. Mr. Fletcher lost his regular cook for a few days and apparently it's hard to hire temporary help. He knew that Pearl had gone away . . ."

"How did he find out?"

"He practically said good-bye to her this morning," Gwen said. "It was a dead giveaway."

"Just because somebody takes an interest in your well-being . . ."

"Mr. Fletcher doesn't give a hoot about my well-being."

"I'm talking about me," Dennis finished obstinately. "Who the devil cares about him?"

"My feelings exactly." Gwen decided to take the offensive. "Tell me, have you ever met a woman named Sherry Crane?"

If Gwen had hoped to startle him, she was doomed to disappointment. A platoon of waiters descended at that moment to remove salad and service plates before offering the main course. By the time coffee had been brought, as well, Dennis had plenty of time to formulate his reply.

Evidently too much time because he calmly started

in on his chicken and Gwen had to repeat her question.

"Sherry Crane?" He didn't sound impressed. "She sounds like a television starlet."

"She looks good enough to be one. If you like peroxide blondes who wriggle when they walk."

"Doesn't every man?" Dennis sounded amused as he put down his fork to butter a piece of roll. "What did this Sherry Crane ever do to you?"

"Not a thing. I just met her yesterday. She's occupying the villa next to ours along with a man named Stanton Brown who's just a little bit too good to be true." Gwen toyed with a piece of chicken, pushing it absently into some lemon sauce by the rim of her plate. "I could swear that I've seen Sherry before. I thought it was one of those days when I drove in to visit Pearl in the hospital."

"You mean in Montana?" Dennis's lifted eyebrows were visible even above the frame of his sunglasses. "Your imagination's running away with you. I admit the name sounds a little familiar . . ." His voice trailed off as he snapped his fingers. "Of course! Your aunt said something about her last night. I'd forgotten until now."

So much for hunches, Gwen thought dispiritedly.

"And from your description," he went on, "I doubt if this Sherry whatever her name is—"

"Crane."

"Sherry Crane," he continued, "I doubt if she'd be running around a small town in Montana in the dead of winter."

"It was just a few weeks ago, but you're probably

right." Gwen decided that she'd had enough to eat and pushed her plate away.

Dennis speared his last piece of chicken and chewed it with every evidence of enjoyment. "Why all this interest in two people you'll never see again?"

"According to Mr. Fletcher, I'll be seeing them at dinner. *If* he lets me out of the kitchen." Her grin was impish. "Do cooks have equal rights at dinner time?"

Dennis remained unperturbed, putting his knife and fork carefully at the edge of his plate. "I don't know. Invite me to dinner and I'll eat in the kitchen *with* you. That way, I can get a glimpse of this fabulous Sherry at the same time."

"Sherry would like the idea but I don't think you're Stanton Brown's type. He's short, stout, and prissy. Not the kind to welcome any competition."

"Who cares? I'm very accomplished as a dinner guest."

"I know." Gwen started to chuckle as she thought about it. "It might liven things up, at that."

"Well, then . . ."

"But you'd better wait until tomorrow night. By then, I can tell Lance—that is, tell Mr. Fletcher . . ."

"You'll choke if you keep trying to call him Mr. Fletcher," Dennis informed her coldly. "And it isn't necessary; you've convinced me that things are on a business basis. But I think I'll still come around to watch the action."

Gwen told herself that it wouldn't hurt for Lance Fletcher to get a good look at Dennis. And for Dennis to see Sherry. Despite everything, the woman still struck a niggling chord in her memory. It was a pity that she hadn't discussed it with her aunt before she left.

" . . . if that sounds good to you?"

Dennis' query brought Gwen from her daydreams in a hurry. "I'm sorry," she apologized. "If what sounds good?"

"A drive up toward Indian Canyon after we're finished here. Or we can take a ride on the aerial tramway if you'd rather. The view should be good in this weather."

She smiled gently. "I don't imagine you got much rest last night after that stint in the hospital emergency room. Why don't you just take it easy today? And that's not an attempt to 'mother' you," she added hastily. "It just makes sense. Besides, I should really go back and see about fixing dinner."

"At *this* time of the afternoon?"

"Well, not immediately," she said, hoping to placate him. "There was a buttermilk pie on the menu here that I'd like to research first."

He nodded reluctantly. "Okay, I'll let you get away with it today but you can tell that landlord of yours that you'll be busy every afternoon for the rest of the week."

Dennis reissued the ultimatum when he dropped her in front of the villa forty-five minutes later. "You should have your head examined," he added irritably, as if for good measure. "We could be getting on a flight to Las Vegas right now. I don't know who you're hoping to impress with this domestic routine."

She reached up to pat his uninjured cheek. "At

least I know where *not* to go for a reference. You'll feel better tomorrow."

"You sound just like my mother," Dennis said, capturing her hand and dragging her close. "Thank God, that's as far as the resemblance goes."

Gwen didn't offer any resistance to his angry kiss, but when he raised his head and tightened his clasp on her waist to prolong the interlude, she shook her head. "Remember your condition. Do you want to borrow our ice bag for your eye?"

His lips came together in a straight line of displeasure as he observed her calm demeanor, obviously unaffected by his kiss. "Well, you won't need it—that's for sure. I'm beginning to wonder if any man can thaw that frigidity of yours."

She took a deep breath and turned toward the door. "I don't know. It might be better if you gave up trying."

He caught her arm before she'd taken more than a step. "Hell! I'm sorry, Gwen. Can I see you tomorrow?"

"Let's see how things work out. Thank you for lunch."

"You're not going away mad?"

She shook her head "Just going away. I hope you feel better. If I don't poison all the dinner guests tonight, I might invite you to sample the fare tomorrow."

His expression cleared. "I'll count on it."

She waited for him to drive off before unlocking the door. As she started over the threshold, she noticed an envelope in the wrought iron mailbox. She ripped it open as she went into the villa, closing the door behind her.

Lance Fletcher's signature was bold and black at the bottom of the typed note and her pulse rate speeded up unaccountably over his words.

> Couldn't reach you by phone, and wanted to let you know that you have the night off. Sherry reports her boss is out of town and she's dining with a friend. I'll be back around eight but the enclosed key fits my front door (in case you want to check out the kitchen, etc., for tomorrow).

She dug the key he mentioned out of the bottom of the envelope and then read the message again. Afterwards, she tucked it in her purse and hefted the key experimentally. Somehow, the idea of prowling through his empty house smacked too much of prying. There wasn't anything magical about his kitchen that couldn't be learned later on, when he was there.

She stuck the key with the note in her purse before going upstairs to change her clothes. There wasn't any reason to hurry and, momentarily, she regretted having sent Dennis on his way. Then she shook her head as she realized that it was really the best thing.

That parting kiss had emphasized what she'd known all the time, and if she wanted to preserve any kind of friendship, she'd have to handle future encounters delicately.

She changed into a pair of shorts and a matching

aqua sun halter before going into the bathroom and running a comb through her hair. Staring at her reflection, she decided Dennis' last taunt of frigidity might have some truth in it. Most women of twenty-four had fallen in love at least three or four times. "And you haven't managed anything more than a crush on that professor who taught undergraduate history," she told herself in the mirror. "Not only that, it only lasted until midterm when he started growing that ratty-looking beard."

At that point, her common sense reasserted itself. People didn't fall in love to order, and certainly Dennis wasn't very smitten or he would have acted differently, too. Which made the whole thing ridiculous.

The sound of falling metal came from the pool area and Gwen pulled back a bathroom curtain to peer down. A short, partly bald man dressed in sober black had picked up an aluminum lounge chair from the poolside and was carrying it back to the patio of Stanton Brown's villa. When he'd placed it near an umbrella table, he straightened and surveyed the area with a satisfied expression. He lingered only long enough to adjust the tilt of the sun umbrella and then disappeared into the house.

Yet Stanton Brown was out for the day and so was Sherry. Gwen let the curtain fall back in place, as she thought about it. Housebreakers didn't stop to move patio furniture, for heaven's sake. Nor did they wear neat black suits and white shirts, surely. On the other hand, housemen did. Especially housemen who doubled as chauffeurs.

Gwen picked up her sunglasses and started down

the stairs toward her own patio, wondering why nobody had mentioned the man before. She'd have to ask Lance about it the next time she saw him.

It wasn't until she'd stretched out on the gaily flowered lounge and was relaxing in the warmth of the sun that she wondered if Sherry might have chosen a new chauffeur for the day. Or was it coincidence that Lance was among the missing, too? He'd said that she was dining with a "friend," which covered a multitude of possibilities.

If the pudgy man in the black suit reappeared, she might find some of the answers, she told herself drowsily. And if her technique worked with a chauffeur, she could try it on Stanton Brown the next night.

That was as far as she allowed her thoughts to wander, but she was well aware that Lance Fletcher was figuring in them—even though she kept him pushed far back.

By the time she finished sunning herself and went in to see what was in the refrigerator, her aunt phoned to report their safe arrival in Phoenix.

"I hope that you're not going to have too much time on your hands—being there alone," the older woman said when she'd told Gwen the phone number and address where they were staying. "Louisa called Dennis a few minutes ago, but there wasn't any answer."

"If that's a roundabout way of asking if he's here, he isn't," Gwen replied in some amusement. "Maybe he's just not answering the phone."

"That might be it. I'll tell her so she won't worry."

Gwen felt an instant's sympathy for Dennis. "Well, he was all right when I saw him for lunch. When he phones tomorrow, I'll mention that Louisa's trying to get in touch." She hung up a few minutes later and went back to survey the interior of the refrigerator with less enthusiasm than usual. The temperature was still high enough to make her lazy. She had just settled on a salad accompanied by iced tea when she realized suddenly that she was preparing to spend another riotous evening in front of the television by herself. Maybe it was a good thing she'd accepted Lance's job offer. At the rate things were going, *anything* was bound to be an improvement.

Her bedside clock showed midnight when the sound of voices down by the pool area woke her from a restless sleep. After she identified them as belonging to Sherry and Lance, she got up and closed her window with a noticeable thud. She hoped they *did* hear the slam—people who had no respect for others deserved such treatment. At least she now had confirmation on the identity of the "friend" with whom Sherry had spent her evening.

Gwen shook up her pillow vigorously before getting back in bed. She could only hope that Sherry had ordered the most expensive thing on the menu for dinner—at least getting a part of her rent money back, one way or another.

Chapter Four

Sleep, when it finally came, wasn't particularly deep or relaxing. Gwen endured dreamlike sequences of being frozen in a solid block if ice while Sherry appeared in her minuscule bikini. She was floating on bundles of money in the pool and Lance rang bells alongside proclaiming her—proclaiming her what? Gwen stretched on the mattress, only half-awake, and discovered she was still hearing bells. It took another ten seconds for her to realize that it was her phone ringing on the bedside table and she flopped over to make a dive for the receiver.

"Hullo . . ."

"Your aunt knew what she was talking about," said a deep masculine voice. "I thought I'd have to use dynamite."

Gwen blinked and pushed upright, almost losing the receiver in the process. "Who *is* this?" she asked cautiously, although she had a very good idea.

"Your friendly landlord and current employer. At least I presume you're still working for me."

"Yes—" Gwen swallowed and tried to think rationally, wondering if she'd suddenly gone speechless because she was only half-awake or whether it was the effect of that voice on the other end of the wire. "Yes, of course. Why? What time is it?" She squinted at the bedroom window, trying to judge the rays of sunshine spilling onto the carpet and then realized that she was freezing in the blast of air conditioning. She sneezed resoundingly in the middle of Lance's reply and had to say, "I'm sorry. What was that again?"

"I said that it was nine-thirty. How can you catch a cold in Palm Springs?"

"I haven't caught a cold—it's just this blasted air conditioning."

"That's easy—turn it off. Most people do at night."

There was a pause while he could have been remembering the slam of a certain bedroom window and Gwen certainly was.

She spoke up hurriedly, instinctively going on the defensive. "I don't know why you're upset. There wasn't anything about my having to cook breakfast, was there?"

"Not that I remember. This isn't business—I just thought you might like to see some of the sights around here before you get tied down this afternoon. Unless you have something else planned?"

Gwen recalled all her uncharitable thoughts when she'd heard him chatting with Sherry at midnight. Evidently he'd decided to spread his considerable charm to another villa for the day. Or maybe Sherry was simply unavailable.

"Hey!" His voice was sharp in her ear. "Have you gone back to sleep?"

"Of course not." Gwen had a firm, businesslike refusal all mapped out, and it was a distinct shock to hear her own voice saying, "I'd like to see some of the places I've read about—if you have time."

"Well, we could speed things up if you'd invite me for breakfast. I have banana muffins to contribute and there's a grapefruit fresh off the tree."

Gwen had trouble sounding calm and sensible. "If I supply the bacon and coffee, I think we're in business."

"Fair enough. How long do you need?"

"I have to get dressed . . ." That time there was no hiding the breathlessness in her voice.

"Twenty minutes?"

She was already starting to strip back the sheet. "Twenty minutes should be fine. See you then."

Always before she'd been a woman who liked to move slowly first thing in the morning, but during the next fifteen minutes she managed to shower and scramble into a pair of designer jeans plus a crisp white shirt. Brushing her hair took just another minute as did the hasty application of powder and lipstick. Afterwards, she surveyed her makeup critically. Just enough was important but nothing was worse than too much at that hour. Satisfied, she moved quickly back into the bedroom, taking time to turn off the air conditioning and throw open the controversial window.

The sound of footsteps below by the poolside

brought an involuntary smile. "Idiot," she told herself softly but sneaked a last look at the mirror before heading for the stairs.

She heard Lance's rap on the sliding glass door as she started down. Her steps quickened and she called, "I'm coming," as she caught a glimpse of his tall figure waiting outside.

The next instant she gave a startled shriek as she tripped and plunged forward, completely off-balance. Instinctively she clutched for the banister, but her outflung arm only managed to keep her head from hitting the uprights as she thumped and tumbled down the carpeted risers, ending in a heap at the bottom.

She lay there stunned, only vaguely aware of the patio door being shoved open with a thud. A moment later, Lance was beside her on his knees, saying in a rough voice, "Don't move. Just stay there until I can find out if anything's broken."

Gwen groaned and rubbed the most convenient ache, which happened to be an elbow. "You don't have to worry. I don't think I'll ever move again."

His hands were moving over her rapidly. "Where do you hurt?"

"It would take too long to tell you." She managed to lever herself against the wall and gingerly felt her neck. "I've never thrown myself at a man before. You should feel flattered."

He scowled at her. "Keep that up and I'll think that you landed on your head."

"I know very well where I landed." She rubbed the spot ruefully. "Believe me, it's not my head."

For the first time, a glimmer of a smile flickered

over his serious countenance. "You *must* be okay. Shall we try getting up?"

Gwen's eyes crinkled with laughter even though she was hurt in more places than she wanted to count and her hands trembled as she braced herself against the wall. "I don't know about you, but *I'm* going to try. No, I can manage by myself . . ."

"Stop trying to act like an Amazon," he told her, brushing aside her objections and helping her to the couch nearby. "Just sit there while I go get you something hot to drink—it'll help calm you down."

"This isn't necessary—I'm perfectly all right."

"Of course you are, but you're bound to feel a reaction after a tumble like that." His voice was soothing and he patted her shoulder like an old friend of the family. "Coffee or tea?"

"You should be working thirty thousand feet up . . ." she broke off as she saw that he wasn't going to relent. "Coffee, I guess. But I feel foolish just sitting here and letting you work."

He didn't deign to answer that, simply going over to the patio door and reaching for a paper bag on the ground.

"What on earth," she began, mystified as he carried it back in, and then remembered. "Oh, I see! Your part of breakfast."

"Exactly." He grinned as he started toward the kitchen. "I dropped it when I saw you take that header. It's a good thing that grapefruit don't break. I'm not too sure about the muffins."

"I'm happy that you weren't bringing eggs. Are you sure that I can't help?"

"Only by sitting there and keeping quiet."

He didn't emerge to enforce his edict, but Gwen didn't risk countermanding his orders. She leaned back against the couch cushion and took a deep breath, trying to relax.

Lance was back shortly after she heard the kettle whistle, this time bearing a steaming mug. "It's instant coffee," he said, sitting down beside her and handing it over. "I've plugged in the percolator but I thought you could use something right away."

"Thanks." Gwen was pleased to note that her fingers only trembled a little as she clasped the handle of the pottery mug. "This should do the trick. Did you have some?"

"I can wait." He pushed up from the couch again and stared at her intently. "The color's coming back to your cheeks. How are you otherwise?"

"All right." She made a rueful grimace. "My elbow's going to be sore along with a couple of other places, but I really got off lucky. I was just lying here wondering how you managed to rescue me so fast. Is there a passkey to that patio door, as well?"

He shook his head, puzzled. "I thought you'd left it ajar for me. You mean that you didn't?"

"I hadn't even been downstairs this morning. I must have forgotten to lock it last night." She pressed the warm mug against her cheek for comfort. "Although I could have sworn that I checked everything before I went up to bed."

"No matter." He started back to the kitchen. "At least I was able to get in just now. Would you like some eggs with your bacon and muffins?"

"No, thanks. Actually I'm not very hungry."

"You'll feel better with breakfast inside you.

Besides, you'll need your strength for sightseeing later on."

"You just want somebody to cook dinner tonight."

"Exactly. You can play the interesting invalid all forenoon but tonight I expect results," he announced from the kitchen. "Finish your coffee and then come on in—the grapefruit's on the table."

Gwen cheated a little and made her way to the breakfast alcove before Lance had taken the bacon from the frying pan. She smoothed her hair nervously as she pulled back a chair and sat down, hoping that she was still presentable after all that had happened.

Lance must have been reading her mind because he said, "You look fine. If I'd taken that tumble, I'd probably still be stretched flat out."

"I owe it all to the quality of carpet and sponge rubber pad underneath," Gwen replied, trying to lighten the atmosphere.

"All kidding aside, that stair carpet was just put down earlier this week. But if it's that easy to trip on, maybe it should be changed."

Gwen watched him turn to take the bacon from the pan, draining it carefully on a paper towel before transferring it to a plate. He brought it to the table along with a pan of warmed muffins and sat down across from her.

She picked up her spoon and started in on her grapefruit. "Did you really pick this off the tree?"

"That's where they come from." He looked amused as he followed suit. "You make it sound like a minor miracle."

"It is—to people who live in snow country. Any-

74

how, it's delicious. Do you suppose I could pick some?"

He pretended to consider it. "Only if you let me come along. With your luck, you'd probably forget to duck, and getting hit in the head with a grapefruit from the top of a tree isn't a laughing matter."

She looked at him quizzically, the spoon halfway to her lips. "You're serious?"

"Absolutely. It might be better if you stuck to oranges."

"Oh, not that. You make me sound like a disaster area." She swallowed the last segment of the juicy fruit and put her spoon down on the edge of the saucer. "The next thing you'll be putting a bell around my neck. Can I be trusted to pour the coffee?"

"Make sure you put it in the cup." Lance was eyeing her humorously. "Right now, you look tempted to pour it down my neck."

"Don't give me ideas."

"You will admit that you seem to lead an exciting life," he said as he pushed the plate of muffins within reach.

"Falling in the pool that first day could have happened to anybody," she said coldly. "You don't have to make me sound like a monster from outer space."

He grinned and picked up a strip of bacon, holding it thoughtfully between his thumb and forefinger. "Well, your luck's bound to change. And, after surviving that plunge down the stairs, I think it already has."

She nodded, as she chewed a bite of muffin. "It's strange that the nap on that carpet didn't bother me before." She stretched out a neatly-shod foot. "I even have flat heels on. You'd think it would have happened yesterday when I was wearing pumps."

"It's hard to tell. Just be grateful for small favors—" he broke off to yawn mightily. "Sorry. I didn't get all the sleep I needed last night."

If he thought that she was going to mention that she knew it—that she'd heard him cavorting around the pool with Sherry at midnight—he was wrong. Gwen decided all that in the short time that it took her to butter another piece of muffin. "I slept very well," she assured him.

"It's a good thing. By tonight, you'll be aching in muscles that you didn't know you owned." He frowned as he thought about it. "You're not going to feel like fixing dinner. I'll explain to Stanton and Sherry and we can all go out."

"That could be expensive for you."

"Not me—my uncle," he corrected, dusting his fingers on a napkin and shoving back his chair. "But he'll be getting off easy. You could sue him."

"For falling down the stairs?" Her lips curved in a fleeting smile. "What makes you think I won't?"

"My God, I didn't mean to give you ideas. Will you settle for a steak dinner instead?"

She started to laugh. "I may wait and count my bruises before I make up my mind."

"Fair enough." He sobered rapidly. "I still intend to pay you for taking Chen's place. There are lots of things you can do besides cooking for the next few days so you won't have to worry about losing the salary."

He sounded so concerned about her finances that Gwen almost confessed then and there that she wasn't dependent upon her aunt for money, and that she really didn't need the extra income. Apparently after hearing that she'd helped Pearl keep her affairs in order during the hospital stay, he'd gotten the idea that it was her steady job. Probably he was extra sensitive on the subject of salary because his own job depended on his uncle's generosity. She sighed as she thought about it. No man wanted to hear that he'd hired a woman whose bank balance was extremely healthy. And if the truth be known, also owned part of the bank.

"What's the matter?" Lance asked, only aware of her sigh and not the real reason for it. "Feeling rocky? Maybe you should be taking it easy."

"I was just wishing I could manage another muffin," Gwen said, lying valiantly. "I've been eating the clock around ever since I arrived. Dennis took me to a wonderful place yesterday," she continued, making an effort to change the subject. "Sort of Spanish style—down in Rancho Mirage. Do you know it?"

"That fits the description of half the restaurants around here." His eyebrows drew together. "This Dennis, was he the one who was driving your aunt?"

"That's right. Dennis Carlton—he's a friend from home. Aunt Pearl went to Phoenix with his mother."

"But he's still here?" Lance had schooled his tone by then, keeping it carefully noncommittal.

" 'Fraid so," Gwen said, responding in the same vein. "He'll probably be over this afternoon. If you don't mind, he might join us for dinner. I told him about Sherry."

Lance shoved back his chair and got to his feet. "The more the merrier. She should enjoy it."

"But what about Stanton Brown?"

"What about him?"

"You know what I mean. Will the extra competition bother him?"

"I doubt it. Sherry's been well trained; all he has to do is drop his checkbook and she comes running."

"That's pure male chauvinism!"

"I don't deny it. On the other hand, it's true." He started moving dishes over to the counter by the sink. "Why is it that women object to the truth if it hurts?"

"Maybe we're brainwashed in infancy." Gwen stood up and carried her coffee cup across. "Do you want to 'fight till six and then have dinner'?" When Lance stared as if she'd taken leave of her senses, she explained. "I'm quoting Lewis Carroll. Tweedledum was a favorite of mine."

He chuckled and unplugged the coffeemaker. "I thought you'd really come unglued."

"Not officially. Don't bother with those dishes. I can do them later. If you're serious about wanting to go out this morning."

"Of course." He stacked the last saucer and dried his hands on a paper towel. "Have you been to the Living Desert Reserve?"

Her face lit up with interest. "No, and I'd love to see it. Aunt Pearl said it wasn't far from here."

"Just down the road toward Palm Desert. We can stop for lunch someplace afterwards . . ." His words trailed off as his glance went toward the window which overlooked the patio. "Sherry," he said flatly.

"She's on the way over. What's that?" The last was to Gwen, who'd muttered something before remembering that ladies didn't use words like that.

"Nothing. I was just surprised." She took a deep breath and walked out to slide aside the patio door. "Hi, neighbor! Come in and join us. Would you like some coffee?"

"Why, yes! I'd love some." Sherry beamed as she came over the threshold. Her smile focused on Lance. "You're staying, aren't you?"

"At least long enough to say hello," he said, rallying to wave her toward the couch. "You're looking particularly good this morning. Isn't that right, Gwen?"

"Lovely!" At that moment, Gwen felt as if her smile was going to crack, so she headed toward the kitchen, saying over her shoulder, "One coffee coming up."

As she plugged in the percolator again, she was thinking that Lance was right; there was no faulting Sherry's appearance at the moment. Her gray sheared terry dress had a halter top, revealing the secretary's smooth tanned shoulders and throat. In addition, there were red espadrilles, which exactly matched the narrow leather belt cinching her trim waist. When the ensemble was put together with her platinum hair, Sherry would have attracted any man within shouting distance. That certainly included Lance, Gwen decided with a quick look toward the other room. He was practically hovering over the couch.

She managed a pleasant expression as she brought out the coffee a little later. "I hope that isn't too strong. There are banana muffins that Lance furnished—if you'd like something to go with it."

"Oh, I couldn't," Sherry protested, smoothing the belt at her waist as she spoke.

Gwen noticed that Lance's glance was instinctively drawn by the movement. "That's too bad—you're missing a treat."

"I know. Anything from Chen's kitchen is good," Sherry informed her. "It's just our luck that he's taking time off right now."

"Don't worry, Gwen and I will make sure that you don't starve." Lance walked over to the patio door, leaning against it as if he had all the time in the world. "Has Stanton left you holding the fort?"

"All day." Sherry grimaced as she spoke. "I thought he came here for a vacation but I was wrong. He's meeting business associates this morning and has scheduled something for later on."

"Don't you have to take notes?"

Gwen's question was perfectly straightforward, but Sherry swung to face her, almost spilling coffee in the process. "Not today—but I can do it perfectly well. Stanton never complains about my shorthand. My typing's pretty good, too."

"I'm sure it is," Lance interposed in a soothing voice. "Gwen just wondered if you were going to be busy. You see, we were planning to visit the Living Desert Reserve this morning . . ."

" . . . and we hoped you could join us," Gwen said, picking up his cue. Managing to sound as if she meant it was even more of a triumph.

Sherry considered it, her eyes narrowed to

thoughtful slits. "Well, it's different. I don't get many invitations to things like that."

Her ingenuous confession thawed the ice that coated Gwen's manner. "I don't know anything about desert reserves either, so we can pool our ignorance. And if we get tired of being educated . . ."

" . . . you'll be in the majority," Lance cut in. "That means I'll spend the rest of the morning waiting for you to inspect all the boutiques in Palm Desert."

"Don't worry, I can do that at home," Sherry smiled, secure on familiar ground. "It'll be nice to see something different."

"A woman after my own heart," he assured her, brightening perceptibly. "Just sit there and drink your coffee while I bring the car around. Unless you want to get a hat or something."

"No, but I'd better leave a note so Stan and Max will know where I've gone." Sherry took a last hurried swallow of her coffee and got up to leave. She lingered on the threshold of the patio, looking appealingly toward both of them. "It won't take long—don't go without me."

"Wouldn't think of it," Lance assured her. "I'll be waiting out on the drive with the car." He glanced at Gwen. "How long do you need to get ready?"

"Ten minutes should do it."

Sherry looked as if Christmas had come early. "Doesn't this sound like fun! I'll be out there."

Lance waited until she was past the end of the swimming pool before he turned to Gwen. "You don't mind, do you?"

After seeing the amazing change in the other

woman's personality, Gwen was able to say quite truthfully, "No, I'm glad she's coming along." She hesitated before adding, "She's different when you get to know her."

He nodded. "And when she's away from her boss. She may be good at shorthand, but I get the feeling that he pays her salary just so he can have her around in a bikini."

"When I saw her at the hairdresser's she was really playing the *femme fatale*. I must say, she impressed the men in the place." Gwen started to carry the coffee mug back to the kitchen but lingered to ask, "Were you properly dazzled when you came to pick her up?"

The vestige of a grin lightened his face for an instant. "She gave up when she found I was just a remittance man. Sherry's very practical."

"Women often are. Did she decide it right off, or was it during your discussion by the pool at midnight?"

He pretended to wince. "I was afraid we woke you up. Actually, I just ran into her when I went out to get a breath of air. I have to take some financial records to my uncle's tax man later this week and I'd been wrestling with figures most of the night."

Gwen's aches and pains suddenly ceased to bother her. So he hadn't been wining and dining the blonde secretary; his note had meant exactly what it said!

It wasn't any trouble to keep her voice light as she commiserated with him. "Getting ready for a session with an accountant is almost guaranteed to give anybody a headache."

"And speaking of headaches"—he looked concerned suddenly—"if you're going 'round the Reserve you should have a hat on. The sun's hot out there. You've had enough excitement this morning without getting sunstroke as well."

"All right." She started toward the stairs. "I have one up in the closet."

"I'll go halfway with you," he said, falling in beside her.

"To inspect the scene of the crime? I expect that I was just careless." Despite her words, Gwen hung onto the stair railing as they went up. "It must have been about here."

Lance bent down to check the deep-piled carpet as she moved on past. "Right. Take your time. It won't hurt Sherry to wait a few minutes."

At the top of the stairs, Gwen stopped to look down at his tall figure. "I meant to ask you . . ." she said hesitantly and then went on with a rush as he looked up to meet her gaze. "Who's Max?"

For an instant he seemed puzzled, then his expression cleared. "The one Sherry mentioned? He's Stanton Brown's driver and houseman. Maybe cook and butler, too."

"Then he must have been the man moving the patio furniture last night. Short, sort of bald, and wearing a black suit?"

"Sounds like the one. He fades into the background. I'll be damned . . ." The last came as Lance glanced down again and put his hand on a piece of carpet in the middle of the stairs. "Here's the culprit. There's a tear all along this step."

She came back down to peer where he was pointing. "Good lord! I really made a shambles of it. I'm surprised that flat heels could cause such havoc."

"So am I. I'm wondering if the fellow who laid the carpet forgot to finish a seam—except that there's no need for a seam in that spot."

"And besides, Aunt Pearl and I would have noticed it first thing. We've been up and down ever since we arrived," she said starting for the second floor again.

"Unless it was glued and came unstuck." Lance sounded as if he were talking to himself.

"That's a possibility." She paused in the upper hall. "You could check with the firm."

"Don't think I won't." He straightened and shot a piercing glance her way. "In the meantime, stay away from that step! You won't forget, will you?"

"It's engraved on my memory. And several other parts of my anatomy," she assured him, rubbing her derriere ruefully. "Otherwise I'd slide down the banister the rest of the time."

He grinned and went on down the stairs, saying over his shoulder. "I'll see you in the car. Don't forget your sun hat."

Gwen lingered just long enough in her bedroom to comb her hair and unearth the hat in question. It was floppy white cotton with a narrow stitched brim, but at least it would afford some protection from the hot rays of the desert sun. She pulled it on, and grimaced at herself in the full-length mirror. "Casual" was the only word to describe her outfit, but there wasn't time to change into something more appropriate. At least the jeans fit nicely and her shirt had retained its starched crispness. They were a far cry from Sherry's bandbox ensemble, but she hadn't planned on a Miss Universe competition when she'd gotten up that morning.

She stuffed her key and some money in a clutch purse before going downstairs again. When she came to the section of ripped carpet, she stepped carefully over it, uttering silent thanks that her escapade hadn't ended with really serious consequences.

Sherry and Lance were waiting in the drive at the side of a sedate mid-sized beige sedan. Gwen's lips twitched as she surveyed its sober appearance, having guessed that Lance would have chosen a more flamboyant model. Then she recalled that a manager's salary—even in Palm Springs—couldn't be very high. She had no reason to criticize the man because he wasn't driving the latest sports model.

Lance was watching her approach with narrowed eyes. "You look as if you're working out an answer to the world's problems."

"Or trying to remember something that you forgot," Sherry put in lightheartedly. "Would you rather ride in front with Lance? There isn't room for all of us and I don't mind the back."

"We can take turns," Gwen said. "Either that or we could make Lance get in back and we'll take over."

He held up his car keys. "Possession is nine tenths of the law. Let's get going before I weaken and head back to the swimming pool—it's going to be in the nineties today." As he opened the rear door, he said to Sherry, "Watch your head—there isn't a decent back seat in this thing. Dammit to hell!"

The last came when a car turned into the drive

and pulled up behind them with a flurry of gravel. Dennis was immaculate, as usual, in a dark blue knit shirt with a beige collar which complemented his cotton slacks. He didn't lose any time getting out from behind the wheel. "What's the deal?" he demanded of Gwen. "Didn't we have a date?"

She opened her lips to protest and then made a helpless gesture. "I'm sorry—I thought we left it up in the air. It doesn't matter now that you're here," she added hastily when she saw his jaw harden. "Sherry, you haven't met Dennis Carlton—a neighbor of mine at home. Sherry Crane."

Surprisingly, the other woman didn't react to Dennis' handsome presence in the way that Gwen had anticipated. Her "hi" was casual to the extreme, and Dennis, although his glance didn't miss one inch of Sherry's measurements, sounded stiff as he acknowledged, "Miss Crane—it's nice to meet you."

Gwen frowned and struggled on when nobody else did anything to break the silence. "And this is Lance Fletcher."

Dennis gave a cool nod as he turned toward Lance to shake hands. "You're the manager of this place?"

"For the moment." Lance didn't sound like a remittance relative then; his appraisal was just as offputting as Dennis'.

"*And* my employer for the moment," Gwen echoed, keeping her voice light but letting her eyes telegraph a warning to Dennis. "We were just going to see the Living Desert Reserve."

"In this heat?" Dennis' brow shot up quizzically. The mannerism wasn't particularly effective because his eye was still bruised, so instead of appearing dis-

86

dainful, he merely looked as if he'd lost a ten-round decision. "Whose idea was that?"

"We took a vote," Gwen interjected, before Lance could say anything. "It isn't far away, so if you'd rather wait here by the pool . . ."

"By myself?" From Dennis' tone, she could have been prodding him to walk a plank over shark-infested seas. "What about our date?"

"We'd be glad to have you join us." Lance's voice was resigned; he clearly wanted to get going and would do anything to put the show on the road. "There's room in the car for four."

Dennis' expression as he surveyed the modest back seat showed what he thought of *that* suggestion. "I've a better idea. We can take two cars—it'll be more comfortable. Gwen will ride with me and help navigate while Miss . . ." He hesitated and looked over to Sherry. "Crane, was it?"

"That's right." Abruptly she turned her back on him and got in Lance's car.

"Oh, for heaven's sake, call her Sherry," Gwen said, nudging Dennis and wishing she could hit him over the head instead. He'd never acted like such a stuffed shirt before—heaven knew why he was doing it now!

Lance reached in his shirt pocket to pull out a pair of sunglasses and put them on. "Okay. We'll meet you in the parking lot at the Reserve." He opened his car door but lingered to ask Dennis, "I gather you know how to get there?"

"No problem." Dennis replied, clearly pleased that he'd managed to rearrange the tour to his liking. "You might as well go on in. Its too hot to wait in that parking lot. Gwen and I will catch up with you by the gift shop or the gatehouse."

His glib assurance didn't convince Lance, who lingered by his car to check with Gwen. "Is that what *you* want?"

Under his steady gray glance, she was hardly conscious of the other happenings around them: the noisy little birds swooping overhead into the palm fronds along the drive, the stifling gusts of a breeze that didn't feel like a breeze at all—even the muted traffic noises which came from a highway hidden by high walls and oleander hedges.

It was Dennis' restless movement which made her realize they were still waiting for her answer. "You don't have to make a production number out of it," he said, unhappy at her hesitation. "Anybody would think that you were being abducted."

She smiled to put his mind at rest and told Lance lightly, "There shouldn't be any problem. The Reserve isn't big enough for us to get lost, is it?"

"Only if you made a special effort on one of the wilderness trails. We'll see you at the entrance then. Don't forget to wear that hat."

Gwen and Dennis had driven only a block toward the main road when he said, "What made him think he had a right to give you orders? Why didn't you tell him to take a hike?"

"Lance was just concerned because I fell downstairs this morning," she said, making light of it.

"Did you hurt yourself?" He gave her a frowning sideways look.

"Tomorrow I might match you bruise for bruise. But there's nothing really serious."

"How did it happen?"

Surprised at his concern, she shrugged. "We found a tear in the stair carpet. I'm not sure, though, whether I caused it or the installer left a seam open. It's a good thing Aunt Pearl wasn't around—if she'd taken a tumble, it could have been bad. Speaking of our dowagers, did you hear from them today?"

"Mother called this morning—they're having the time of their lives." Dennis didn't linger on that subject, going doggedly back to the other. "You'd better watch your step. When you're not familiar with a place, you can get in a hell of a lot of trouble."

"Home accidents, you mean? They can happen anywhere." She frowned when he didn't reply. "Surely you're not hinting at anything else? Just because we've both had a run of bad luck recently."

"Of course not," he said with a snort. "There *is* such a thing as coincidence. "I'm just telling you to be careful. If you'd come to Las Vegas with me, you'd be in better shape now," he finished triumphantly.

"Maybe. Who knows? The wings might have fallen off the airplane."

"The way things are going, I think we'd both better keep our feet on the ground and stay out of dark corners."

The last was uttered in a dead level voice and Gwen knew that he meant every word he said.

Chapter Five

Dennis' warning was another disconcerting setback in a morning which had already had more than its share.

After the pronouncement he kept his attention on the heavy traffic, but even if he hadn't, Gwen doubted that he would have said any more. It wasn't the first time that he'd chosen to drop a dramatic bombshell into their conversation, but it was hardly justified then. Surely he couldn't be making a major villain out of the foolhardy driver who'd run him off the road. She shook her head and promptly dismissed the possibility. At least he'd forgotten to remind her of his elopement proposal when he'd mentioned Las Vegas, confirming her opinion that it had been prompted by finances rather than unrequited love. Her bank balance had attracted more than one suitor in the past—one reason why she was secretly delighted that Lance thought she lived on her aunt's largesse.

It wasn't quite fair not to set the record straight. On the other hand, there wasn't a good way to say, "Look, I don't really need any extra pocket money so you can forget about finding a job for me." It was especially difficult since he wasn't in the same enviable position.

"For somebody who's supposed to be interested in local scenery, you're doing a good imitation of a zombie." Dennis' comment sliced ruthlessly into her thoughts. "Are you sure you want to go on with this jaunt, or shall we give it a miss? They'll get the drift when we don't show up."

She shook her head and then winced, wishing she hadn't been so vigorous. "Lord, no! Don't forget that Lance is my landlord—if we pulled a trick like that he'd cut off the electricity or something."

"Just because we left him alone with that blonde?" Dennis' lips twisted wryly. "He'd probably lower your rent."

Gwen rested her head against the back of the seat and stared out at a new shopping center as they pulled up at a red light. Like all the suburban malls which dotted the sides of the highway to Indio, it was thronged with cars and people—laughing, light-hearted people who were obviously enjoying their holiday in the sun. Which was more than she was doing at that moment.

"Did you hear what I said?" Dennis asked as the light changed and he stepped on the accelerator again.

"You came through loud and clear." Gwen moved

her head to glance his way. "It's not surprising that Lance likes her—Sherry's a pretty spectacular dish." She paused as he swung the car off on a bougainvillea-lined boulevard which wound through an expensive town house development and then added, "You weren't very charming. Are you off all beautiful blondes this week or just ones named Sherry?"

"I love one named Gwen," he said, "but I'm having trouble getting the idea across. Would you like it better if I made a pass to keep my hand in?"

"Nope. I would just like to enjoy a civilized tour of this place," she gestured as he turned in a drive where a sign board proclaimed the Living Desert Reserve. "Afterwards we might even have lunch." She pulled on her cotton hat as he slackened speed in the crowded, dusty parking area and finally braked in an empty space. "How does that sound to you?"

"Do I have a choice?" he asked, showing a rare flair of humor.

Gwen simply got out of the car, knowing that he really didn't expect an answer to that. The blast of heat that met her when she'd opened the door had taken her breath away, anyhow.

Dennis swore under his breath as his hand touched a hot piece of metal in locking the car. "I hope your friend Lance plans a short tour in this heat. If I'm going to bake, I'd rather do it beside a swimming pool or hanging onto a gin and tonic." He took her elbow, urging her toward a shaded entrance complex at the end of the lot beyond some tour buses.

"At least there are lots of trees around here," she said, trying to find a cheerful note. "I wonder where

Lance and Sherry are—I don't see them by that glass doorway."

"They'll be around." Dennis put an arm around her shoulders, drawing her close as they went up the cement walk. "It doesn't matter to me if we never find them—I'd rather be alone with you." He pulled her to a stop just outside the door and tipped up her chin with his other hand. "All you have to do is say the word—" He broke off to bring his mouth down on hers with a possessive gesture that caught her completely unaware.

Not for long, though. She pushed back from his clasp, emerging breathless and red-cheeked with embarrassment. "For heaven's sake!" she muttered, seeing the stares of a tour bus group getting their entrance tickets. Flustered, she put up a hand to push her hair back from her face and became aware that something was missing.

"Is this what you're looking for?" It was Lance's cool voice as he came up behind her, offering her white cotton hat.

Gwen snatched it from him as if it were red-hot, stuffing it in the back pocket of her jeans. "Thank you, it must have fallen off when . . ." Too late, she found where her treacherous tongue had led her.

Lance didn't waste any time on diplomacy. "Exactly. Next time you'll have to get something that ties under your chin." He turned to Dennis and handed him two tickets. "I've already taken care of the formalities—you can go on in. Sherry's waiting at the gift shop off the patio."

Dennis smiled but kept a possessive hand at Gwen's elbow as they started through the gate.

"You're wrong about that—she's right over there, watching for us."

"Perhaps you'd take one of these maps," said a pleasant, gray-haired woman wearing a badge that showed she was a Reserve volunteer. She gave each of them a yellow sheet indicating the paths around the Reserve, adding that there was a Visitor Survey on it they could fill out. "If you have time," she added with a smile.

Gwen's cheeks flamed under her benevolent look. Obviously the woman thought that she and Dennis were so engrossed in each other that the displays would come in a poor second.

Fortunately, they encountered Sherry before any other comments could be made. She'd been sitting in the shade of a palm but there was nothing cool and relaxed in her manner. Instead, she was almost aggressive as she confronted Dennis. "You certainly must have taken the long way around. We've been here for ages." She turned to Lance, saying, "Let's go down and see the birds. I heard some people talking about them."

Lance glanced at the other two. "Is that all right with you?"

Gwen spoke up quickly before Dennis could object. "It sounds fine. I like aviaries and it's on the main path, according to this map."

Lance's formidable expression smoothed at her words. He nodded and started off ahead of them, Sherry hanging tightly on his arm.

The two of them didn't waste any time as they passed the various exhibits of trees and shrubs at the side of the path. Gwen would have liked to stop and read the explanatory plaques for the gray smoke tree or the red-blooming Baja Fairy Duster, but there was no chance if she kept up with the party. Even if she could have lagged behind Lance and Sherry, there was no hope of escaping Dennis. He kept a firm hand at her elbow and surveyed the various exhibits with a glazed, resigned expression. He *did* pull up on the path when some quail crossed in front of them, but only because Lance and Sherry's immobile figures forced him to. Gwen took a moment to appreciate the scurrying birds before concentrating on some low-growing dyeweed which was planted next to the more common saltbush.

"Look, why don't you take Sherry and go on to the aviary?"

It was Lance's voice addressing Dennis as he came back toward them. "Some of these desert plants are fascinating, and I'd like to spend a little time inspecting them. It looks as if Gwen's interested in them, too. There's a lath house over here with some experimental stuff . . ."

Since he was leading her toward it as he spoke, Gwen couldn't do more than grimace over her shoulder to Dennis, left frowning on the path. Her last glimpse was of him turning abruptly to Sherry and gesturing her toward the towering aviary near the end of the Reserve.

"I thought that might do the trick." Lance spoke with some satisfaction as he hurried Gwen along. "Other than turning his back on Sherry completely, there wasn't much that your Lover Boy could do."

"Now look here—he's not my . . ."

"Lover? Don't tell me you're 'just good friends' after that display of his by the entrance. He must have known that you wouldn't object or he wouldn't have tried it in the first place."

Gwen pulled up on the path, her eyes flashing with temper. "I *didn't* know what was going through his mind or I would have stayed home. Honestly, between the two of you . . ." She rubbed her forehead distractedly.

"Go on." His tone hadn't changed. "You were saying?"

"That you're giving me a miserable headache."

"Really." He looked sternly down at her. "Which one?"

"What do you mean?"

"Which one of us is giving you the headache?" As he saw her take a deep breath to tell him in detail, he relented. "All right, I'll stop badgering you, but in my opinion Dennis doesn't add much to the gathering. Of course, he obviously puts forth extra effort where you're concerned."

She waved that aside. "I've been thinking—he didn't make any passes until we reached the front entrance. *Almost* as if he wanted a public place to . . ." She searched for the right words.

". . . make sure that everybody saw him stake his claim?" Lance narrowed his eyes as he thought about it. "I wonder why?"

She shook her head. "Not everybody. Just you or Sherry."

He started walking again slowly, his attention ostensibly on the planted borders. "More likely both. I can understand why he's telling *me* 'hands off,' but he doesn't seem like the kind to exhibit dislike toward a good-looking woman. Incidentally, Sherry reciprocates the feeling."

"And she isn't the type to act that way when a presentable man is introduced."

"Exactly," he agreed, stopping in the shade of a rampant-growing palo verde, spectacular with its yellow blooms. He reached up to pull Gwen's hat more squarely on her head. "I'm not surprised you have a headache. Haven't you anything better than that?"

Gwen pushed her hat back to its original angle. "It's all right, I had the headache earlier. Don't change the subject. What about Sherry and Dennis?"

"I'd bet next month's salary that they've met before, that's all. That's why I thought they needed a chance to be alone."

"Oh, I see." So much for her hopeful conclusion that he'd had his own reasons for wanting to visit the lath house. Gwen rubbed her forehead again and decided that she really could use some aspirin.

"You shouldn't be wandering around here in this heat," Lance said, showing that her action hadn't gone unnoticed. "When I first mentioned the idea, I was thinking of a quick tour before going on to a good air-conditioned restaurant for lunch. I sure as hell didn't plan on it working out like this."

"I'll be fine as soon as I take an aspirin or two. Do you suppose there's a drinking fountain back by the gift shop?" She cast a wistful glance down the other way, where the upper confines of the aviary could be seen in a palm grove. "There's an animal care center down past the bird enclosure I really wanted to see."

Lance took her arm and started along a curving walk toward the front entrance. "We'll come back another day. I doubt if Dennis and Sherry are in the mood for a prolonged excursion, either."

Gwen felt better at the prospect of imminent air-conditioning. Another comforting fact was Lance's tall figure at her side. She shot an upward glance at him and was relieved to see that his features were relaxed again; apparently his anger at Dennis' actions had faded. "It may sound ridiculous to you, but I thought that I'd seen Sherry somewhere before, too. She does make quite an impression," Gwen announced solemnly.

"You can say that again."

"Saying it once is all I can manage. There's such a thing as carrying good sportsmanship too far!"

He bent his head to administer a deliberate appraisal, from her toes up to the brim of her hat, not missing an inch on the way. "Sherry's quite a dish, but she isn't in your league. What's more, you know it." He didn't wait for a response before going on. "Where did you see her before?"

"I'm not sure that I did."

"Okay. When you *thought* you saw her. Was it here?"

She shook her head. "It was at home—one day when I was visiting Aunt Pearl in the hospital. I even checked with Dennis about it. He generally keeps tabs on the good-looking women around town."

"And?"

She shook her head. "It didn't ring any bells, but

he might have been away on a skiing trip about then."

Lance rubbed his jaw with the edge of his thumb. "Probably we're imagining things. But if we're not, it's quite a coincidence that they've both surfaced on the same territory. And why Palm Springs right now?"

Gwen spotted a drinking fountain near the entrance and slowed to search for some aspirin in her purse. "I could have Aunt Pearl ask Louisa—Dennis' mother. It might be worth a try."

"Here, let me hold that." He took her purse from her as she tried to juggle it and open the "childproof" cap on the aspirin container at the same time. "Even Einstein would've needed two hands for one of those." He waited until she'd swallowed two pills with a drink from the fountain before handing her purse back. "Do you want to sit on that bench over there or go in the gift shop where it's cooler?"

"The bench is fine," Gwen replied, starting toward it. "What do we do when Dennis and Sherry show up?"

"I know what I'd *like* to do, but I'd get arrested if I tried it." Lance sat down beside her and stretched long legs out in front of him. "Maybe you'd rather just go home."

"The aspirin should work in a few minutes and I'll be fine," Gwen told him hastily. She chose not to add that if she went home Dennis would probably supervise her convalescence. "Is there a good place to eat around here?"

Lance rested his arm along the back of the bench,

idly tracing the shoulder seam on her blouse. "That depends. Do you like French pastries?"

Her eyes lit up. "Adore them. Especially whipped cream Napoleons."

"My Lord, a soul mate! You should have told me before. Why were we wasting time talking about . . ." He stopped and pretended to think. "What *were* we talking about?"

Gwen knew better to answer that truthfully. Just then Lance was looking at her without a touch of icy reserve. Instead there was laughter in his voice and his finger had moved to lightly trace the outline of her ear. His deliberate touch made her take a deep breath and she could only hope that the thundering of her heart wasn't visible through her cotton blouse.

Then the sound of footsteps on the cement walk reluctantly brought their attention to more practical matters. They turned to see Dennis and Sherry approaching, each stony-faced and silent.

Lance uttered a muffled groan and got to his feet. "That must have been the quickest tour of the aviary in history," he muttered to Gwen before turning to greet the newcomers. "We were just discussing lunch. Shall we wait for you in the car or are you ready to leave, too?"

"I was ready twenty minutes ago." Dennis bit the words out as he came across to hover by Gwen. "How about you, honey? Did you get tired waiting?"

"We weren't gone *that* long," Sherry said, addressing his back.

If they were going to act that way, Gwen

thought rebelliously, even a whipped cream Napoleon couldn't save lunch.

Evidently the same idea occurred to Lance. "We haven't been waiting long," he told Sherry in a no-nonsense tone, "but we might as well get going. Gwen and I decided on a place called Michel's on Palm Canyon Drive."

"I know where it is," Dennis announced, taking Gwen's elbow as she stood up. "We can meet you there. The place is usually crowded at lunch time, so we'd better not hang around here any longer."

Lance's expression didn't give anything away. Instead, it seemed to Gwen as if he'd resigned himself to the circumstances, knowing there was nothing he could do to change them.

And there wasn't, she realized. Not without alienating both Sherry and Dennis. "We'll meet you there, then," Gwen told him.

Lance nodded slowly. "I'll take time to phone a reservation. That way we'll be sure of a place."

"I'll go with you," Sherry said, making it clear whose side she was on.

Dennis turned abruptly toward the exit and urged Gwen ahead of him. "Crazy blonde," he muttered as they got outside the gate and were walking down the inclined walk toward the parking area.

"Present company excepted, I hope."

"What's that?" He scowled and then managed a half-hearted grin. "Naturally. I was talking about her."

"Translated to mean Sherry?" Gwen hurried past the exhaust pouring out of a tour bus. "Anybody would think that you'd taken a path to purgatory instead of a simple walk to an aviary." She slowed her steps to add, "I've heard of instant replay and instant coffee, but instant dislike—that's ridiculous!"

"I know." He seemed to be thinking his next words over carefully because they'd almost reached the car before he uttered them. "Actually, we *did* meet before. At home, that week before I went away skiing."

Gwen's features took on a look of satisfaction, but she kept the triumph from her voice as she waited for him to unlock the car door. "I gather that she made quite an impression on you."

"Why do you say that?"

"Oh, for heaven's sake, Dennis! Don't be so starchy! The list of women in your address book would stretch from here to that aviary back there and I've never seen you do anything but ooze charm around them."

He pulled open the car door with a jerk. "That charm didn't do much to convince you."

"You really weren't putting your heart and soul into it. Probably because you were afraid I'd take you seriously. And don't bother to deny it," she said, as she got into the stifling car. "Whoosh! It must be over a hundred in here."

"It'll cool off as soon as I get the air-conditioning going."

He slid behind the wheel and turned the ignition key. There was a low groaning noise from the engine that brought instant dismay to their faces.

"Hell—a dead battery! That's all we need," Dennis said, striking the steering wheel with his fist. "Damn rental cars!"

"There's no hope for starting this one without help—that's for sure." She looked around at the crowded parking areas. "At least we're not sitting by the side of a deserted highway."

"Just roasting in a dirt lot." He yanked the key out of the ignition. "Well, I'll call the rental agency and roast some parts of *their* anatomy. Do you want to stay here or go with me?"

"Something wrong?" came a male voice.

They'd been so intent on the car troubles that neither Dennis nor Gwen saw Lance until he was beside the car.

"The agency fobbed a sick battery on me," Dennis said, making an effort to control his temper. "I'm going in to call for another car."

Lance nodded but made no effort to move away. "Unless you feel strongly about it, why not phone from the restaurant? They can deliver the new one wherever you want. It would help—you and Gwen won't have to sit here cooling your heels." He grinned suddenly. "I think I picked the wrong cliché—there's nothing cool around here."

"You're right about that," Gwen said quickly getting out on her side. "The restaurant sounds like a fine idea. That way Dennis can complain in comfort at an air-conditioned pay phone.

Dennis got out of the car. He didn't look happy but he had little defense against such a convincing argument. "I'll be along as soon as I leave these keys in the glove compartment."

The dead battery was enough to command token courtesy when they all converged on Lance's car. Even though there wasn't much room in the mid-sized sedan, everyone was scrupulously polite about suddenly being jammed together. Even Sherry and Dennis contributed to the general discussion which followed, centering mainly on the weather ("That damned smog from L.A. gets closer all the time") and the traffic ("a few tourists from out-of-state cause most of the accidents"). The latter comment came from Lance and brought heated denials from the other three, lasting until they'd parked in downtown Palm Springs and entered an attractive restaurant. It was a light, airy place with white wrought-iron tables, cheerful waitresses, and an air-conditioning system that didn't specialize in freezing blasts. Even Dennis' mood improved noticeably after he'd made his call to the rental agency and been promised quick delivery on a replacement.

Lunch was better than expected and the desserts were fabulous. By the time they'd consumed the luscious whipped cream Napoleons topped with sliced strawberries, they could barely manage to sip espresso coffee and reflect on their good fortune.

It was Sherry who surprisingly offered a suggestion for the rest of the afternoon. "I want to go up the tramway," she said, sitting straight in her chair and surveying the others. "I've wanted to ever since I heard we were coming here, and I don't know when I'll have another whole day off."

"What's the matter?" Dennis drawled. "Doesn't that boss of yours know about the forty-hour week? Or do you get a nice bonus for overtime?"

"Stan treats me very well," Sherry said, her chin going up. "I'm not complaining about my working conditions."

"I'll bet," Dennis put in.

She continued, her cheeks fiery. "I just don't want to waste my free time."

"Thanks very much." He pulled an imaginary forelock. "I've been accused of lots of things but that one slipped by."

"You know what I mean. Besides, it's no business of yours." Sherry sounded ready to cry as she turned to Lance, sitting beside her. "If you don't want to go—or Gwen—I'm sure that I can find other ways to get there. Max would have driven me except that he was busy."

"With your boss, no doubt," Dennis added.

"That's right. It isn't surprising since he works for him. Just the way I do."

Lance cut in before the dispute could escalate. "Tell you what—I can't go up the mountain today but I can drive you to the tram station and pick you up later. Will that do?"

Sherry flushed with pleasure, as if she weren't used to people making an extra effort on her behalf. "You're sure you don't mind?"

"Not a bit." He turned to survey Gwen's quiet figure. "How about you? Do you feel like a breath of mountain air? The upper station is located at eighty-five hundred feet."

Gwen tried not to shudder visibly. Even if she'd been feeling tip-top, an aerial tramway ranked along with chocolate-covered grasshoppers and marinated rattlesnake on her list of things to avoid. She cleared her throat and tried to be diplomatic. "I'd better get back home and start planning dinner. Not that I can compete"—she gestured toward a serving cart full of pastries nearby—"but even a simple menu needs homework."

Lance opened his mouth as if to contradict her but then reached for his glass of water instead. Dennis looked around almost angrily before tossing his napkin on the table. "I'll go along with you," he told Sherry.

"You don't have to . . ."

"I know that." A faint smile crossed his features. "If I stay at the villa, Gwen will probably have me peeling potatoes. Besides, some of that cool mountain air would feel good."

He didn't even hint that he'd enjoy spending the rest of the afternoon in Sherry's company. It was such a deliberate maneuver that Gwen suspected he wasn't as opposed to the idea as he claimed. And as for peeling potatoes, she doubted that he knew how to find a paring knife, let alone use one. Nevertheless, it was best to support his declaration. "Now I'll really have to get organized," she told Lance in pretended dismay. "I'd planned on making Dennis do the grocery shopping as well as K.P."

Sherry bit her lip at that, blurting out her next words impulsively. "I'm sorry. I didn't mean to cause any trouble. There'll be other times to take that tram ride—"

Lance's laughter interrupted her. "Don't believe everything you hear. If Gwen needs help, there'll be plenty around."

"Heavens, yes!" Gwen decided to confess. "Besides, I'd gladly peel potatoes if it would get me out of an aerial ride. My toes start to curl if I'm on anything higher than a kitchen stool."

Dennis turned abruptly to face her. "My God, was that why you cried off on flying to Las Vegas!"

His exclamation brought frowns to both Lance and Sherry's faces. Gwen observed their changing expressions and could have groaned aloud. Just when things had been starting to get halfway civilized, Dennis had managed to muddy the waters again.

"I didn't know you'd planned a trip to Nevada together," Sherry began, her voice rising. She faced Dennis accusingly. "You've got a real genius for changing your mind. *And* your women."

Lance shoved back his chair and got to his feet, stopping the discussion even before their waitress could hurry over with the check. By the time Dennis had offered to pay and Lance had overruled him, Gwen had hustled Sherry out to the front door.

"Dennis just made that offer of Las Vegas to help fill time while his mother was in Arizona," she told the blonde, keeping her fingers crossed behind her jeans. "He likes to gamble and wanted company while he was at the tables. Sitting here in the sun appealed to me more."

"Then the plane ride . . ."

". . . didn't have anything to do with it." Gwen was able to tell the unvarnished truth on that. "And for pete's sake, take him with you on the tramway today. He wouldn't have offered if he didn't really want to go."

"You think so?" Sherry sounded almost pathetic in her eagerness to believe.

"Think what?" Dennis asked suspiciously, coming up behind them.

"That I'll take a nap when I get back to the

villa," Gwen replied without hesitation. "This heat makes me sleepy and that tremendous lunch didn't do anything to help."

"It sounds like a good idea," Lance confirmed, joining the party as they left the restaurant. "I'll drop you off first and then take the others out to the tramway."

"Do we have to make reservations or anything?" Sherry wanted to know when they were walking to the car. "And how will we get back to town?"

"The cars go to the summit stations every half hour," Lance said. "Once we get out there, you can decide when you want to come down again. Gwen or I can pick you up at the valley station then. It's only a few miles out of town so there's no need to worry."

His calm demeanor set the tone for the drive back home. A surge of traffic on the main highway out of town didn't appear to bother him in the way that it had infuriated Dennis earlier. Lance even found time to point out the attractive barberry shrub borders at the base of the towering palms which gave the street its name. Gwen followed his lead, commenting on the display windows of the stores and specialty shops until they reached the Villas' driveway.

Sherry decided to hurry in and pick up a sweater after hearing that she'd need one at the summit of the tramway ride.

While she was getting it, Lance walked alongside Gwen to her door, saying, "I wasn't kidding about your taking a nap while I'm gone. You still look under the weather."

"Whatever happened to the unobservant man?" Gwen wanted to know, disconcerted that nothing escaped his eagle eye. "I wasn't fooling about having to do some preparation for dinner. Unless you'd settle for bacon and eggs—and I can tell you from experience that Dennis won't."

"I'm sure you can." There was a dangerous undertone to his voice as he pulled up at her doorstep. "An invitation to Las Vegas usually indicates more than a casual relationship, even these days. I wasn't aware that your friendship"—he snapped the last word off as if it were distasteful—"had progressed that far."

"If I wanted that kind of 'friendship,'" Gwen told him, echoing his tone, "I could have it right here or at home. And before you decide to have me paraded through the streets, remember that I turned him down." She stared at him crossly. "What's happened to everybody? I think this heat addles your brain."

Evidently her annoyance was more convincing than she thought, because an almost sheepish expression came over his lean face. He shoved his hands in his pockets, as if unsure of what to do with them. "Maybe you're right. Anyhow, I haven't changed my mind about your getting some rest this afternoon. There's a chance that Chen will be back."

"But you said he had some days off . . ."

"Just take my word for it, will you? I'll explain later. You'll be here?"

"Of course."

She must have looked as bewildered as she sounded because he smiled suddenly and ran a finger lightly down her cheek.

"Cheer up. Ten years from now, you won't remember a thing about it," he said. "There's Sherry joining Dennis—I'd better get them on that tramcar before they declare war again. I don't know about you, but I feel like a referee thrown between the Christians and the lions when they're around." He let his hand drop to his side again. "If it keeps on, I'm going to take out some extra insurance. See you later."

Gwen waved the three of them off somewhat absently. As she went in the house, she reached up to touch the skin he'd caressed and then blushed as she caught sight of herself in the hall mirror.

"Don't be foolish!" she told her reflection severely. Flirting came as naturally to Lance as breathing. He'd probably showered Sherry with compliments the times they were alone. Anything to keep his guests happy.

Putting her clutch purse on a convenient table, she went on in to the television alcove, which seemed especially restful when contrasted with the bright sunlight outside. She turned off the air conditioning and opened the patio door to get some fresh air before collapsing on the big davenport. The cushions were even more comfortable than she remembered, and she shoved a small triangular pillow behind her head as she put up her feet and settled herself against the arm.

The possibility that Chen would be back to prepare dinner took that worry from her mind. And if the cook were back, it would be silly for Lance to try and justify an extra salary. She'd have to tell him in a firm, but tactful, way that she'd be glad to help for free. She yawned as she thought about it and burrowed more comfortably into the cushions.

It seemed only an instant later that there was a shrill ringing in her ears. She groaned a protest and pushed herself up, unsure exactly where she was. Or, more important, where the phone was that was ringing so stridently. When she finally discovered it on a table nearby, she scrambled for the receiver.

"Hullo . . ." she managed, her voice thick with sleep.

"I can tell that you took my advice."

It was an instant before Lance's meaning registered. Then she squinted at the watch on her wrist and drew in her breath. "Good Lord! It's almost five! Have you been ringing forever?"

"Not long. I hope you'll notice that I'm being especially tactful. When Chen does the early-morning calls he just says, 'Hello! Get up!' in a very firm voice."

"Is that because his English is thin?"

"Not at all. Apparently they did it that way in a hotel in Hong Kong where he worked. It's effective, believe me."

"We live and learn. I take it that he's back in your kitchen," she asked, trying to sound as if it really didn't matter one way or the other.

"That's right. I picked him up after I dropped Dennis and Sherry at the tram station. Since you don't have to worry about dinner, how about coming with me when I pick them up? I'll have to leave in a half hour."

"I'd like to."

"Good. I'll be out in front when you're ready."

Gwen didn't waste time after she hung up the receiver. In the half hour he mentioned, she managed to shower and change into a raspberry and white printed sundress which she wore with high-heeled sandals. She surveyed the finished result with satisfaction and went carefully down the stairs. This time, Lance wouldn't need to play nursemaid again.

From the flash of admiration that went over his face as she emerged from the front door, a chaperone role was farthest from his mind just then. He whistled softly before opening the car door for her. "I didn't know a two-hour nap could accomplish all that!"

Color stole up her cheeks at his fervent compliment. She tried to think of something bright and sophisticated in reply and, as usual, found herself entirely speechless. She could only smile as she stepped into the car, uttering a soft "thank you" as he closed the door.

It wasn't until they started down the drive that she discovered he was in an open-throated white shirt worn with the sleeves rolled up his forearms and a pair of gray gabardine slacks. She started to smile and he turned his head to catch her at it. "What's the joke?" he asked.

"Now I know why so many stores down here sell clothes. In this weather, everybody must change outfits three times a day."

He laughed, turning his attention to the traffic again as they reached the main highway heading into town. "Except that the natives don't wear many clothes when the temperatures are in the nineties—like today."

She nodded. "I feel sorry for people without air conditioning. Standing over a hot stove wouldn't be a joke around here. That reminds me—"

"Chen is standing in an air-conditioned kitchen and feeling no pain, if that's what you're worried about," Lance said, cutting in.

"He can't be very happy at having his holiday interrupted. How did you know where to find him?"

"That wasn't hard. Whenever he has a day off, he heads straight for the Sick Duck. His cousin owns it."

"The Sick Duck? What in heaven's name is that?"

Lance's shoulders shook as he chuckled. "Sorry. I forgot that you're a newcomer. There are two Chinese restaurants in this part of town with 'Duck' in the name. One's by the airport and the other's near the hospital. The one by the airport became known as the 'Flying Duck' . . ."

"And the other one became the Sick Duck. It makes sense, I suppose." She considered it thoughtfully before saying, "I only hope that nobody opens another one next to a mortuary."

Lance let out a shout of laughter. "You'd better mention it to Chen tonight—in case his relatives are thinking of expanding."

"You mean it will be safe for me to go into the kitchen? I thought he'd take after me with a cleaver at least."

"Why? It wasn't your fault that you fell down our stairs. Incidentally, there'll be someone from the carpet company to repair that step tomorrow." He shot her a sideways glance. "You didn't suffer any permanent damage?"

"Certainly not." She yielded to impulse; putting one thumb in her ear and another in her mouth, as she mumbled "Can't you tell?"

He grinned and pulled her hand down on the seat between them, covering it for a moment in a firm, possessive clasp. "All I know is that you're a different woman from the one who tangled with the patio umbrella. She was definitely frosty around the edges. On the other hand . . ." he paused, letting the silence lengthen.

"Yes?"

"They were mighty choice edges."

His grin broadened as she pulled her hand away, pretending more irritation than she felt. "There speaks the expert," she announced. "I noticed you were appraising Sherry's bikini a little later."

"All in the line of duty," he declared solemnly. "Considering the rates we charge at the Villas, a conscientious manager is a downright necessity. And speaking of Sherry . . ."

"That's what I'd call a deft change of subject."

"You're the one who brought her up," Lance reminded. "At least she's a pleasant change from some guests who think that a hefty bank account is all that's needed in this world."

Gwen winced inwardly, hearing the scorn in his voice. There was no reason for her to take the criticism personally, she told herself. As far as Lance knew, she earned far less of a salary than Sherry. Nevertheless, it was going to be harder to confess that she really wasn't her aunt's chauffeur/secretary the way he thought.

"Most of the guests at the Villas are nice, obliging

souls though," Lance was continuing. "We look forward to seeing them each season. Especially the ones who trip over holes in the carpet and don't complain."

"I'll call my lawyer tomorrow and tell him to skip the litigation. What about Sherry? Will she get a return invitation?"

"As long as she packs a bikini." His tone sobered suddenly. "That's a strange friendship she has with Dennis—if you could even call it that."

Gwen gestured in dismay. "I meant to tell you about that. Dennis admitted that he'd met her before. In our hometown—of all places. Although it's strange that his mother didn't mention it to my aunt."

"Not really. Sherry isn't the type that a man would take home and introduce to his relatives."

"That's not very charitable."

"I was trying to be realistic. The way she was earning her living didn't change Dennis' mind about her, though. Not in the long run. A psychiatrist could have a field day with that love-hate relationship. By the time they come down from the tram ride, they should have their feelings worked out."

"Either that, or only one will come back."

He grinned. "I hadn't considered that possibility."

They were approaching the business district with its one-way streets that funneled the traffic through town. Lance threaded his way along easily, keeping a steady speed except when stopped by a traffic light. Gwen settled more comfortably in the corner of her seat so that she could watch his relaxed profile without being obvious about it.

It wasn't until they were past Racquet Club Road on the other side of town that Lance broke the comfortable silence that had fallen between them. "If Sherry was up in Montana a little while ago, where was her boss?"

"Stanton Brown?" Gwen frowned, trying to remember if Dennis had mentioned the other man. "I haven't the faintest idea. Maybe Sherry wasn't working for him then."

"You're wrong about that. She's been with him for six months. He told me so when they first arrived. Something about it taking that long before a secretary is really efficient."

"Mmmm." Gwen's disparaging monosyllable showed what she thought of that. "Or maybe he was just trying to put a veneer of respectability on their relationship. Not that I don't think she earns every penny of her salary with him," she went on, trying to be fair.

"But you think she earns it for a different kind of talent?"

Gwen wriggled uncomfortably. Lance's tone had been without censure but she wished suddenly that she hadn't said anything.

"I imagine she's been around the block a few times," Lance continued, braking for a left turn at the intersection where a huge sign advertised the Aerial Tramway. "That's why I'm wondering what's going to happen now. Stanton Brown isn't the type to take kindly to competition—either in business or his private life."

Gwen thought about that while Lance accelerated up the two-lane road which climbed steeply to reach the tram's lower station. Just as at the other boundaries of the resort, the lush manicured landscape had vanished like Cinderella's coach as soon as they left the city lots and myriad housing developments. Within a block, green grass turned abruptly to straggly gray underbrush growing on a rocky hillside. Parts of the nearby acreage still bore blackened remains from the last brushfire—the nemesis of California landowners. As the car continued to climb and round the curves, Gwen could look back down onto the city proper dotted with swimming pools, palm-lined streets, and sprawling luxury estates, which transformed that part of the desert into an oasis beyond belief. Almost like the boundary of Shangri-la, where taking a single step meant leaving the ordinary world to enter an enchanted land. Only somehow, the specter of Stanton Brown hovering over Palm Springs put a tarnish on the gloss of resort life.

"Do you suppose he could have had anything to do with Dennis' accident the other night?" she asked finally.

If Lance was surprised by the abrupt question, it didn't show in his voice. "Not personally. Stanton's the type to push buttons and make other people do the dirty work." He hesitated while they went 'round another curve and passed a van that was laboring on the steep grade before adding, "Besides, he didn't have any reason to be unhappy with Sherry then. She hadn't gotten together with Dennis."

"So far as we know." Gwen leaned forward to peer up the road where the tram tower appeared for the first time. Seeing the abrupt rise of the cables to the top of the towering mountain behind it, she sighed with relief that she wasn't having to ride a tram gondola that day. She sat back again as Lance slowed the car's speed but ignored the overflow parking lots at the side of the road.

"We'll go on up by the station to the main lot," he said, taking still another switchback. "Notice how much cooler it is up here?"

They'd kept their windows down to avoid powering the air conditioner while on the steep grade, and at his comment, Gwen nodded. "The temperature must have dropped ten degrees," she agreed. "Sherry probably needed the sweater she took along."

"Even more up at the top of the mountain." Lance was pulling into a steep lot that was crowded with parked cars near the big terminus. "That bunch of people coming this way must mean that a tram has just arrived."

"Where do we meet Sherry and Dennis?"

"I told them I'd pick them up by the entrance." Lance turned off the ignition and pocketed the key. "You might as well wait here—I'll be back in a few minutes. There should be some reading matter in the glove compartment if you're bored."

"Thanks. I'll get out and stretch my legs. What's over the wall?" She indicated a low barricade at the edge of the lot some fifty feet away.

"Saltbush and weeds, I suppose. Why?"

She wrinkled her nose, unabashed. "My pioneering spirit. I'll find out and tell you when you come back."

He grinned and strode off, making his way past the people who were scattering to find their parked cars. Gwen stared after him for a minute and then at the new arrivals. Most of them were parents, complete with tired children. The adults were unlocking doors and issuing a barrage of orders like "Leave your brother alone, Johnnie!" or "This is the last time I take you anywhere until you learn to behave, young lady!" Gwen smiled, remembering similar threats when she'd been that age. Probably she'd deserved every one of them, she decided, as she sauntered over to the barricade to escape the confusion.

A quick check of the hillside below showed that Lance had been right in his guess; there wasn't much to look at except undergrowth and some trees on the hill just beyond the tramway terminus. Her gaze went back up to that awe-inspiring cable ascent. Probably the ride was something she should do later on. Pearl might want to go eventually or Lance might even suggest it if Sherry waxed enthusiastic on the way home.

A shrill whistle brought her head up abruptly and she saw Sherry standing by Lance's car, two fingers to her lips. Gwen waved in acknowledgement, saying admiringly as she walked over, "I always wanted to be able to whistle like that."

"It comes in handy. Especially if you're trying to get a cab in the rain. I never do it when I'm with a man, though." Sherry grinned, gaminelike. "It crushes their ego."

"And speaking of egos—" Gwen glanced toward the end of the parking lot, where the people were still milling about their cars. "What did you do with Dennis? And Lance?" she added hastily, realizing that she'd scarcely been diplomatic.

"They're coming. Lance wanted to get a

schedule." Sherry's cheeks were flushed and there was a glow about her. "Oh, Gwen, the view was simply fantastic! You should have come with us."

"You're right. I feel like an awful coward—especially after seeing all these people." She nodded toward a family group close by. The father was unlocking his car and stuffing a toddler into the front seat while a six-year-old, drinking a can of soda, happily scuffed the toe of his tennis shoe on the pavement.

As Gwen watched them, the father swore loudly, realizing that he'd left something on the tram or lost it on the path. "Jeff, stay and take care of your brother while I go back to look for his sweater," he told the older boy. "I must have dropped it on the walk down. I know I had it when we got off the tram." He ran his hand through his hair irritably and started to retrace his route, leaving the car door open and the two youngsters staring gravely after him. An instant later, the older boy finished his soda and idly dropped the empty can at his feet. It started to roll on the sloping surface of the pavement, making him gurgle with laughter and chase after his new toy. Retrieving it, he came back by the open car door and, stooping, rolled the can toward the rear fender again. "Look, Bobbie!" he shouted in his childish treble. "Watch it go!"

The younger child, who was standing on the front seat, obediently stumbled toward the door to watch, clutching the gear shift lever to keep his balance.

Gwen and Sherry watched horrified as the car rolled backward, slowly at first and then gathering momentum each second. The toddler on the front seat let out a surprised crow as he clung to the wheel.

His childish voice appeared to break the spell. Sherry made a dash for him. Gwen streaked toward the older boy, who, chasing his aluminum can, was directly behind the car as it rolled backward down the sloping lot.

The youngster was bending over to retrieve his prize as she swept up and caught him in her arms, dragging him sideways to safety even as she stumbled and fell. She managed to shield his body in the process and clung to him as they slithered and rolled across the gritty parking lot surface—finally coming up under the back bumper of a car parked next to the road.

There was an instant of stunned silence and then the boy in her grasp let out a wail of protest—not surprising under the circumstances. The next minute, both of them were being hauled unceremoniously to their feet while Lance announced roughly, "God in heaven! It isn't safe to leave you alone even for a minute!"

Gwen was brushing the gravel from her knees and elbows while trying to placate the youngster who was squirming in Lance's grip. "The other boy," she began breathlessly, and then added, "Oh, thank heavens!" as she saw that the car had been halted at an odd angle. Sherry and Dennis were just then handing the younger child to the unnerved father, who looked ready to collapse on the spot.

"Come with me, young man," Lance said, swinging the older boy up in his arms. "You're going back to your family."

"But my can . . ." the boy protested tearfully as he was borne away.

"You can get another one at home," Lance told him.

Gwen remained where she was, still trying to pull herself together. She had a momentary impulse to rescue the empty can if it would soothe the youngster's distress and then saw it under the side of the car—flattened and wrenched out of shape. It was impossible not to remember the sturdy little boy bending over it just moments before who could have suffered the same fate.

Suddenly the trees on the hillside started behaving strangely and the stiffening in her knees gave way. She leaned against the parked car behind her in a desperate attempt to steady herself but realized that it wasn't enough.

In an instant, she'd slithered onto the parking lot again—aware, even as it happened, that Lance was going to be a little late for the rescue once again.

Chapter Six

It couldn't have been more than a minute or two before he was down on one knee beside her, his face as pale as her own. "Why in the devil didn't you tell me you were hurt!" He was running a hand over her shoulders as he spoke, trying to find the problem.

Gwen pushed out of range, and struggled to her feet as she said crossly, "I'm not hurt. Not really."

"Of course not, you just sit on the pavement whenever you get tired."

"Very funny!" She found it a relief to lose her temper since it stopped her tortured imaginings. "I just suffered a little reaction, that's all. And you needn't stare at me as if I didn't have both oars in the water—"

"I wasn't doing anything of the kind—"

"—because I didn't hit my head at all." She rubbed her derriere absently, realizing she *had* hit that part of her anatomy again, plus sacrificed her nylons and a considerable amount of skin. Then a more important thought occurred: "The little boy— he didn't get bruised on the pavement, did he?"

Lance gestured toward the station wagon, being driven from the lot with both youngsters waving happily. "The two of them are as right as rain. Their father aged five years though. He wanted to come over and shake your hand, but I told him it wasn't necessary. I hope you don't mind."

"Heavens, no!" She watched the station wagon turn onto the highway with a feeling of relief and then fell into step beside him, going back to the car. "Sherry's all right, too?"

"A little shaky, but Dennis got in on the rescue faster than I did. Sherry just had to hang onto the toddler while he managed to brake the car." Lance bestowed a frowning sideways glance. "Don't you remember any of it?"

She shook her head. "It happened so fast. I didn't stop to sort it out."

Dennis heard her last sentence as they reached the car where he and Sherry waited. "Another bloody little heroine," he said, beaming proudly. "And if that guy who drove the station wagon has his way, everybody in Palm Springs is going to hear about it."

At his announcement, both Sherry and Gwen groaned in unison. Sherry spoke up first, saying fervently, "Dennis, you idiot! The last thing I want is publicity. You know what Stan will say! Why didn't you do something?"

"Yes, why didn't you?" Gwen seconded. "It wasn't that big a thing, anyway."

"That's a matter of opinion," Lance said levelly, unlocking the car so they could all get in. "I'm sure that father is well aware of how important it was."

"I agree," Dennis said as he helped Sherry into the back seat and then got in beside her. "But I also knew that the last thing you wanted was to see your names in the paper. Fortunately, the poor guy was so unstrung after getting his two kids in the car that he didn't argue when I told him he'd better get them home fast."

Gwen smiled in relief but Sherry expressed her approval by throwing her arms around Dennis' neck and giving him an enthusiastic kiss.

"That's my man," she announced to the others. "Actually, I couldn't have held onto the boy *and* stopped the car, so Dennis really deserves most of the credit."

"You all rate a bottle of champagne," Lance said definitely. "Let me do that part at least."

"Hold the thought," Dennis replied, leaning forward to rest his arms on the back of the front seat when they were underway. "But Sherry and I'll have to take a rain check for the time being. I was just going to ask if you'd drop us at the car rental office downtown?"

"I thought you were picking up your replacement at the villa," Lance said, giving him a puzzled glance in the rear vision mirror.

"Well, I changed plans," Dennis said, sounding slightly evasive. "It's better this way—all the way around."

Which translated to mean that he and Sherry wouldn't be under Stanton Brown's eagle eye when they picked up the rental, Gwen decided. She had her theory confirmed as Dennis added, "We've made other plans for dinner, too—if that won't inconvenience you."

"Of course not. I'll tell Chen when we get back. How was your ride up the mountain?" Lance asked, deftly changing the subject.

"It was great!" Dennis sat back in the seat and draped a possessive arm around Sherry's shoulders. "We wouldn't have missed it for anything—isn't that right, honey?" He shifted to stare fondly into her upturned face.

Gwen didn't miss the obvious adoration that Sherry bestowed in return. Something else that didn't need translating, she told herself, and was surprised to find that the discovery of young love didn't help her mood. "Which is ridiculous," she muttered aloud and blushed when Lance shot her a questioning look.

Fortunately Sherry was oblivious to the byplay. She rested her head against Dennis' shoulder, as if content to finally follow her natural instincts and desires. Even her expression had softened; she looked much younger and more vulnerable, very different from the sharp-edged personality who decorated the side of the swimming pool that first day.

It was also evident that she had no desire to resume her former role. She said wistfully, "I wish we didn't have to stay around this place. My idea of heaven would be to go back to Montana and hide away for a while. At least until Stan gets over being mad because I'm quitting."

"Don't worry, he can't hurt you. I'll make damn sure of that," Dennis promised.

Gwen turned in the seat to add, "And if you really want to take a vacation now—stay where the sun is shining. It's cold up in our part of the world."

"Oh, that didn't bother me. I liked everything about the town when I was there. Even if it is a sleepy little place—it's exactly the right size for settling down."

Which just went to show how misleading a person's outer shell could be, Gwen thought. At first glance, the other's mannerisms and appearance indicated a woman whose mink-lined nest would have to be Manhattan or a choice residential area in Los Angeles. Instead, Sherry was talking about living in a town where at least half of the two thousand residents were beef cattle. On the other hand, there'd never been a mugging in the county, smog was unheard of, and the theater manager doubled as chief of police because he was in town anyhow on Saturday nights.

Gwen smiled at Sherry, saying finally, "If you do come to stay, they'll probably draft you to head the Chamber of Commerce."

"That's all right with me. I owe the place a lot," Sherry confessed, snuggling against Dennis as she spoke. "You know, it's the only time I've enjoyed combining business and pleasure. Stanton wanted me to call on your aunt, and I met Dennis on the same trip."

A frown crossed Gwen's face. "Aunt Pearl didn't say anything about it."

"Oh, that's because I didn't really talk to her. By

the time I learned she was in the hospital, Stan wasn't interested any longer. You see, he'd found that the land by the border wasn't hers at all—" She broke off to give Dennis a puzzled glance. "Why are you looking at me in that funny way? Gwen can understand how we all got mixed up on the deed to that property. It can't be the first time her name has been confused with her aunt's. Isn't that right?"

"We didn't discuss it," Dennis said, sounding ill at ease, even though he kept his arm around Sherry's shoulders.

"But I thought Stan said . . ." Her protest faded as she saw his thick eyebrows come together. "I never could get things straight," she improvised to Gwen a second later. "I don't know why I worry about telling Stan that I'm going to quit. Probably he'll be glad to get rid of me. Maybe I'll even get a bonus. Not that I'd take it," she added after noting Dennis' deepening frown.

Lance had been an intent listener to the conversation, but when Sherry finally fell silent, he said, "Well, I'm glad everything's worked out so well for you. I didn't know that I was doubling as Hymen's messenger when I drove you to that tram ride."

Gwen took pity on the two puzzled people in the back seat. "He's talking about being the messenger for the marriage god. Those crossword puzzles I slave over come in handy now and then."

"Exactly." There was a ghost of a grin on Lance's face. "Where do you suppose *I* learned the expression?"

"Oh, crosswords . . ." Sherry sounded relieved. "I never do them. They use such strange words. All goddesses of fertility or somebody's mother from an island in the South Seas."

"I'll take gin rummy any day," Dennis agreed and leaned forward again. "Just pull up at the end of this block, Lance."

The other braked in front of the car rental agency a minute later and leaned across Gwen to look into the office. "I think the place is closed. Are you sure they were expecting you?"

"The manager promised to stick around until I came. See, he's unlocking the place now." Dennis opened the rear car door and helped Sherry out onto the sidewalk beside him. "Thanks for running a delivery service," he told Lance through the window. "We'll be in touch."

Gwen waved to Sherry and sat back in the seat again as Lance maneuvered out into the traffic on Canyon Drive and toward the Villas. "Well," she said when they'd gone two blocks and he hadn't said anything, "it's been a surprising day."

His lips tightened. "Spare me the polite conversation. You don't have to pretend any longer. I'm just sorry that it turned out this way for you."

She stared at him, completely nonplussed by the sudden violence in his voice. "I—I don't understand. Just because I've skinned my knee a little bit . . ."

"I'm not talking about that. Although you certainly have an excuse to go into a decline after what happened up there."

"Well, then—if it's not that . . ."

"Oh, for God's sake, Gwen—don't play the innocent. Sherry might succeed in using that routine with Dennis but don't *you* try it." He swore and braked suddenly as a car ignored a stop sign at an intersection and cut in front of him. It had pulled into the other lane before he went on angrily, "Just what kind of land deals have you and Stanton Brown been discussing in that home town of yours? I hope you didn't leave the old homestead without nailing things down—considering his reputation."

"I haven't been dealing with Stanton Brown on any of our land—"

"Don't split hairs," he interrupted. "I gather your aunt wasn't interested, but you're still in the thick of things. Even though Dennis did his best to shut Sherry up."

The injustice of Lance's accusation made Gwen's own temper flare. "So I'm tried and convicted without even having a chance to defend myself?"

"You don't have to pull in the Bill of Rights!"

"This is a free country. I can do whatever I damn well please."

"All right, I'll listen to what you have to say," he agreed, sounding reluctant. "Maybe we'd better postpone the confession until we get home—or at least out of this traffic."

"I'll go along with that," she said, sitting stiffly in the seat. "With the way my luck has been going, I'd hate to tempt fate again."

It was in thick silence that they completed the rest of the journey, but Gwen's thoughts were far from quiet. Lance had been like another person ever since the mishap up in the parking lot. Sherry's comments on the ride back to town had been indiscreet but not important enough to bring on this sudden black mood. It was especially maddening that she hadn't told him the truth about her circumstances before, because any explanation now would certainly be found lacking.

She was so intent on the subject that she didn't know he'd turned in the circular drive and braked in front of the villa until he said, "All right, I'm listening."

She moved to face him, aware as he turned off the ignition and the air conditioning that the temperature inside the car was already uncomfortably warm.

"You'd better make it short," he said, pocketing his keys. "Those knees of yours should be washed."

Making her sound like a fugitive from a gravel pit, Gwen thought, as she spared a glimpse at her ruined nylons. Unfortunately, he was right—she *did* look like a disaster area, but rehabilitation could wait. "I'll survive. Besides, I need to clear up some misconceptions. You apparently have me tagged with every crime in the book."

He pointedly addressed a palm tree in front of the windshield. "Why is it that women have to dramatize everything?"

"Because men specialize in leaping to conclusions."

"All right—let's try a few facts. There's a hell of a lot more to Sherry's visit up north than you let on. Now I'm wondering how much you know about Stanton Brown?"

"I just met the man the other day."

"That doesn't prove a thing."

"Will you listen to me, please?" Gwen rolled down the window beside her, feeling that even the warm outside air would help change the charged atmosphere. "Sherry didn't explain properly. My aunt and I had the same initials before her marriage. Actually I was named for her—'Pearl' is just a family nickname. Stanton Brown apparently thought that she owned a piece of land that he wanted to buy."

Gwen had Lance's complete attention by then. "She didn't but you did. Is that right?"

"I guess so."

"So you're not just a poor secretary-bird hoping for crumbs from the family table?"

Gwen winced, knowing that the moment of truth was at hand. "Something like that."

Lance faced her squarely, his gaze level and unwavering. "Why didn't you mention it earlier? Nobody would have thrown you out just because you owned an acre or two of property."

Gwen chewed on her lower lip. She couldn't very well confess that he'd be dismayed even then if he knew that it wasn't acres of land she owned but miles. That was enough to daunt a man with a hefty salary of his own let alone one in his position. She drew in her breath and decided against any further explanations.

Her unhappy expression seemed to moderate Lance's ire. His voice was carefully noncommittal as he opened his door, saying, "You'd better go in and get cleaned up."

"And then what? How do we tell Stanton Brown about Dennis and Sherry?"

"My God, don't you ever learn? That's strictly their business. We don't tell Stanton Brown anything except the weather reports. He's involved in so many rackets that it isn't safe to even mention death and taxes."

Gwen got slowly out of the car, bewilderment on her face. "Well, if that's the case, why did you rent him the villa?"

"I didn't. I mean not personally," Lance said, coming around to close her car door. "The paperwork was handled through a real estate broker. I wasn't here that day."

"Well, next time stick around," Gwen said, digging for her house key as they went up the walk. It wasn't the most tactful remark she could have made, but by then she ached and smarted in more places than she cared to count. Lance hadn't exhibited more than a token amount of sympathy after he'd scooped her up from the parking lot. Earlier she'd had hopes of a cozy twosome on the drive back or, at least, a "kiss it and make it well" gesture, but the determined line of his jaw showed nothing was further from his mind.

"Here, let me do that," he said brusquely, taking her door key from her fingers and inserting it in the lock.

"I can manage," she protested and then subsided as he dropped it back in her palm—as if even the most casual contact was to be avoided at that point.

Her suspicions were confirmed when he said roughly, "I'm sure you could, but as a favor to me—try curbing any extra impulses for a while. Just go in and get cleaned up. I'll call Doc Lane to come and check you over."

"That's absurd. Doctors don't make house calls for skinned knees these days."

"I know that," Lance countered impatiently, "but Lane lives in the next block. Besides, he owes me a favor. After your two nosedives you need an expert opinion."

"But I was going to get cleaned up and help Chen with dinner," she protested. "Even if Sherry and Dennis don't come, Stanton Brown might be there."

"In which case, he'll be fed. Without your help. I'll have Chen bring something over to you after the Doc's come and gone."

Her chin went up as she persisted stubbornly. "Is this a diplomatic way of saying that my services are no longer needed? I thought you had to give notice, even to temporary help."

"Look, I know you're feeling lousy and I'm willing to make allowances, but if you keep on that tack, you'll collect some more bruises on the seat of your pants."

"This is too much!" she sputtered. "Just because I want to know where I stand—"

"If you're worried about job security—which I doubt—you can count this as sick leave."

So now he believed she was mercenary as well as a congenital liar, Gwen thought in despair. "I wasn't worried about the salary," she insisted. "It's the principle of the thing."

"Very commendable. Unfortunately most people can't afford that attitude."

Add "spoiled rich" to her other accomplishments, Gwen concluded. If she had any sense, she'd go inside and close the door before he canceled their lease.

"You don't have to be so sensitive about the job. I'd be glad to do most anything for you," she confessed, letting go of her pride in one fell swoop. "If it would help out."

He stared at her, his expression inscrutable, before he said softly, "Damned if I can figure you out. Either you're incredibly naive or a spoiled little madam who should know better."

"Thanks very much. Either way, I'm irresistible."

"There you go again. Just get in the house before I forget the things my mother taught me about how to treat a lady. And try to stay out of trouble."

Gwen could feel her heart thumping in her breast like a long distance runner's. She tried desperately to control her breathlessness so he wouldn't know the havoc he was causing, but she managed to challenge his ultimatum. "And if I don't?"

He reached out and pulled her tight against him in one decisive movement. His free hand caught the back of her hair, forcing her head up so that she had to meet his demanding gaze. "Then you'll be sorry as hell! Do you need convincing?"

Every instinct told her to move even closer—to let herself finally feel his lips against hers—but feminine pride rebelled. Even so, it was an almost painful effort to say scornfully, "Dennis had more sense than to try to threaten a woman."

Her mention of the other man made Lance step back immediately, with an elaborate "hands off" gesture. "I forgot for a minute that I was competing with your home-town hero."

"Dennis isn't anything of the sort. Sherry's welcome to him," Gwen said, wishing that she hadn't made such a foolish remark.

His shrug was a masterpiece of unconcern. "So much for true love. At least you won't need any help or advice to get over your loss."

Gwen clutched the doorknob, realizing that she'd have to beat a hasty retreat from the argument right then or she'd burst into tears. "You know what I think of your advice . . ."

"Lord, yes—you've made it clear enough." He hesitated, "What if I suggested your spending a few days with your aunt in Phoenix?"

"I'd tell you exactly where *you* could go," she snapped back.

Damn the man! It was all too evident that he didn't miss having her in his arms. Probably he hadn't even planned to kiss her except in the most unpleasant way possible—to prove a point.

Lance's tanned face remained austere, "Then we won't bother to discuss it. I'll have Chen bring your dinner later when the doctor leaves. If there's anything else I can do," he added wryly as he started to walk away, "don't hesitate to let me know."

Chapter Seven

Lance's attitude was enough to send any woman around the bend. Gwen decided that after she'd gone inside and closed the door so she wouldn't have to watch his tall figure strolling down to the drive.

She leaned against the cool wood surface and stared despondently into the quiet living room. If anyone had told her the week before that she'd be on the verge of tears over a veritable stranger, she would have hooted with laughter.

But it was hard to find anything remotely funny in her present predicament. And it was all the more frustrating because her emotions had been swinging like a pendulum ever since Lance had rescued her from that patio umbrella. Their relationship had finally seemed to be flourishing until a few minutes ago, but his last words had put paid to any hopes of a shared future. If her ego weren't already at an all-time low, his bald suggestion that she get out of town and stop bothering him would certainly have put it there.

Gwen walked through the deserted house, taking time to unlock the patio door and shove it aside so that some fresh air could circulate. The poolside was apparently deserted. Three canvas lounges looked inviting in the late afternoon sunshine, as did the clear still water, but Gwen stared at the scene with unhappy eyes and went upstairs to wash away the dust and grime.

At least there were two healthy and happy little boys, she told herself. That was something to cling to—although Lance hadn't spent any time talking about it. It was as if he'd decided to overlook the entire occurrence. Probably the women he usually took out for an afternoon never forgot their eye shadow or suffered a shiny nose. Gwen stared at her scrubbed reflection in the bathroom mirror. "Hardly Palm Springs quality," she told herself and went downstairs to wait for the doctor.

It wasn't long until the doorbell sounded and she found a nice, middle-aged individual standing on the step, black bag in hand.

Dr. Lane listened to her story and then examined her briskly. He told her that she'd probably feel thoroughly uncomfortable from her bruises and left a packet of tablets to insure a good night's sleep. As he stood to go, he suggested that she phone his home if she suffered any negative reactions.

"I'm sure I'll be fine," she said, seeing him to the door. "I really didn't want Lance to call you at all."

"So he told me." The doctor looked amused. "It

wasn't any trouble—we're practically neighbors and I can understand his concern."

Gwen almost told him that responsibility was a more appropriate word than concern but thought better of it.

After the doctor left, it was only fifteen minutes before the doorbell sounded again. This time, it was an elderly Chinese who was carrying a tray full of covered dishes.

"Mr. Lance say to bring your supper," he announced, marching through to the kitchen table without even hesitating. "When you finish, we pick up tray out there." He jerked his head toward the patio. "Okay?"

"Okay—I mean—thank you very much." She peeked under one of the covers after he deposited the tray on the table. "This looks delicious. It will be nice not to have to cook."

He nodded in agreement and departed without another word, choosing the open patio door for his leavetaking instead of going around to the front.

Gwen saw him hurry around the corner of the swimming pool en route back to his own kitchen. A muscular young giant wearing jeans and carrying a skimmer for the water's surface was coming from the utility area at that moment. Gwen frowned, wondering who the newcomer was and then relaxed as he grinned and said something to the cook. Chen barely paused but there was no doubt that he recognized the maintenance man and accepted his presence.

Gwen went back to her own kitchen and sat down to eat. She tried to be discreet in observing the maintenance man's progress at the pool. As he worked, she was interested to see Stanton Brown's houseman appear and talk to him, as well. She wondered idly if Lance had deliberately chosen to stay out of sight for the evening, letting the newcomer take over. "That shows how far gone you are," she muttered irritably to herself.

She made a second cup of coffee when she'd finished the succulent roast veal and ratatouille that Chen had brought. Lance was probably finishing his own meal at that moment, giving thanks that he'd been spared her gastronomic experiments. Not that there was any way to find out—Chen merely wanted a return of his crockery, not a discussion of his employer's living habits.

She washed the dishes, piled them neatly on the tray, and went out to leave them on the patio table. By then, the maintenance man had disappeared, and Max, the houseman, must have gone back to his domicile. At least, there was light behind the closed draperies in Stanton Brown's villa. For an instant, Gwen stood staring, wondering if Sherry had returned to give notice and pack her things. If she had, it was a discreet, quiet leavetaking. There was only a faint breeze rustling the palms to disturb the peaceful twilight.

Around the estates up on the purple-shadowed foothills, scattered sections of outdoor lighting illuminated brick walls and moon gates, Spanish cupolas and Moroccan flat roofs. The residents of southern California were not to be denied their touches of fantasy, Gwen decided. The whole effect was beautiful but unreal, and she wondered what she was even doing there. Feeling sorry for herself, she concluded, and locked the patio door before going resolutely up to bed.

Two hours later, she'd finished three crossword puzzles and a novelette. She'd also managed to thrash around enough so that her bed looked as if a herd of wildebeest had gone through it on their annual migration. It was a situation that called for getting up to pull the bed linen back together again.

Once it was done, she glanced at the clock wearily, wondering how long it would be before she finally felt sleepy. She'd been reluctant to take the pills the doctor had left but decided that maybe she should give in. Certainly she wouldn't prove anything if she spent the night tossing and turning.

It only took a minute to swallow the pill with a glass of water from her bathroom and she detoured on her return to stare out the same window where she'd seen Lance and Sherry the night before.

This time, the scene was quiet and peaceful, with the outdoor spotlights around the pool the only source of illumination. She glanced toward her landlord's darkened windows and experienced the unreasoning but understandable irritation that insomniacs feel against the rest of a sleeping world. Her lips tightened still more when she recalled that it was only since she'd met Lance that she'd had trouble with insomnia. "Which proves exactly nothing," she told herself as she stomped back to bed. "At least tomorrow will be better—that's what it says in all the fortune cookies and horoscopes."

But when she was awakened by her bedside phone at eight o'clock the next morning, she wasn't so sure. It was an effort to surface from her drug-induced sleep and she almost upset the table lamp in trying to find the phone receiver. There was another delay while she untangled the cord before finally getting the phone to her ear.

"Gwen, dear—are you all right?"

It was Pearl's concerned voice, and hope gave way to disappointment in her niece's breast. Gwen felt so guilty at that unbidden reaction that she made her reply more cheerful than usual. "Of course, Aunt Pearl. The phone woke me up and you know what a zombie I am first thing in the morning."

"I'm sorry, dear. I probably should have waited until later but we've been up so long that I forgot that you might be sleeping in."

Anybody who slept past eight o'clock didn't automatically rank as a sluggard or sloth so far as Gwen was concerned, but affection for her aunt made her ignore that fact. "I didn't get to sleep until late," she said briefly. "What's happened? You're all right, aren't you?"

"*I'm* fine. It's Louisa. Gwen, you'll never guess what Dennis has done!"

Her unhappy tone made the last fuzziness in Gwen's mind disappear like dew under a desert sun. "Don't tell me he's killed somebody!"

"What a strange reaction," her aunt countered, after a shocked silence. "Why on earth did you say that?"

Gwen couldn't very well explain that violence went hand in hand with Stanton Brown—and that the last she'd heard, Dennis and Sherry had planned a confrontation. "It was because I'm still half-asleep,

142

I guess. What *has* Dennis done? Surely he didn't have another car accident?"

"I didn't know that you were such a pessimist," her aunt replied severely. "You and Louisa would make a perfect pair this morning. She's been ready to leap off the balcony ever since Dennis phoned to say that he's in Las Vegas with Sherry Crane."

"Is that all? Good Lord, he *is* a grown man."

"That's not the point. He told his mother that he doesn't plan to go anywhere without Sherry from now on. That was the main reason he called."

Gwen sat up straighter in bed, her lips curving in a smile. "Did he happen to mention honorable intentions?"

"That's what made Louisa take to her bed with a cold towel," Pearl reported in lowered tones. "He actually plans to marry the girl."

"Well, bully for Dennis! And Sherry, too."

"You don't sound at all surprised." There was suspicion in her aunt's voice. "What's been going on there?"

"I'll tell you when I see you," Gwen replied. "Are you both coming back or is Louisa going to have her nervous breakdown in Arizona?"

"I don't know. You can't blame her, really. She's never even met the girl!"

"They'll get along fine once everything's settled and Sherry starts buying her clothes a size larger. She's just what Dennis needs."

"His mother has different ideas."

"Louisa isn't marrying her," Gwen pointed out. "The main thing is—Sherry's crazy about Dennis and she wants to make him happy. You might tell his mother that."

"It would have a lot more effect if *you* could."

"What about the happy pair? Aren't they going to appear?"

"Not for a while. Dennis mumbled something about it being better this way."

Which meant that Sherry wanted to stay out of Stanton Brown's range until the heat was off. Probably it was the smartest thing they could do under the circumstances.

"You sound a little unstrung for my favorite aunt," Gwen said finally. "Do you need reinforcements?"

"Darling, *could* you come?"

There was such relief in the older woman's voice that Gwen knew she'd made the right suggestion. Pearl didn't often panic, but her recent illness left her less able to cope with Louisa's dramatics than usual.

"If I leave right after breakfast, I should be there by dinnertime," Gwen assured her. "Do you want me to bring any more of your things?"

"I shouldn't think so. After all, we'll be coming back when Louisa feels up to it. It might be a while, of course."

"All right, I'll tell Lance that the villa will be empty."

There was a pause and then Pearl spoke hurriedly. "If you think it's necessary. You're sure that you don't mind driving such a distance alone?"

"Of course not." That wasn't quite true, but Gwen knew there wasn't any alternative.

"Then I'll go and tell Louisa that you're coming. I knew I could count on you."

Which made it all worthwhile, Gwen told herself as she packed an overnight bag later on. She wasn't looking forward to telling Lance about her change of plans—especially after she'd been so vehement in her refusal to even think about Phoenix when he'd suggested it. It did seem an almighty coincidence that he was getting his wish, even indirectly. And there was no real reason for a personal discussion with him about it. Momentarily, her pride warred with her desire to see him again—whatever the excuse. His mood might have improved overnight, especially once he learned that she *was* leaving town. And if she let him think that he'd made her change her mind . . .

Her chin went up stubbornly as she thought about it. Damned if she'd play such silly games, even to win Lance Fletcher's approval. Let *him* figure out an apology next time!

After such a splendid resolve, it was disappointing to find even *that* had been denied her. She discovered that the young giant who'd been cleaning the swimming pool the night before was sprinkling the parking strip when she finally emerged from the villa, overnight case in hand. Stopping only to make sure the door was locked behind her, she marched down to him. "Good morning. I'm Gwen Lawson."

"Yes, ma'am. Lance told me." The young man clutched the hose tightly with his left hand and extended his right to shake hands briskly. "I'm Pete Noltman." He eyed her case. "Taking a trip, are you?"

His intent tone didn't fit the rest of his demeanor and Gwen squinted against the sun to bestow a closer look. He wasn't as young as she'd thought, and despite his casual garb and the hose in his hand, she had the feeling that he'd learned the gardening business practically overnight.

Trying not to show her disquiet, she reached into the pocket of her madras blazer and handed him the envelope she'd addressed to Lance. "I'll be away for a while. Would you give Mr. Fletcher this note, please?"

"I'm sorry—I can't do that, Miss Lawson."

Her brows drew together. "I'd do it myself except that I have a long drive ahead. It won't take you long."

"That doesn't have anything to do with it." His attention went beyond her as he raised his voice to call, "'Morning, Mr. Brown. Looks as if it's going to be another hot one."

Gwen turned, managing a polite nod toward Stanton Brown, who was standing down the drive, obviously waiting for his car to be brought around.

Pete Noltman didn't let the pause lengthen. He plucked Gwen's case from her fingers and swung it into her car as soon as she unlocked the door. Then, rolling down the window by the driver's seat, he barely waited for her to slide under the steering wheel before closing the door behind her. "I know you want to be on your way."

"But my note—" Gwen said distractedly, equally anxious to get out of the neighborhood before Stanton Brown's car arrived. "I want you to tell Lance . . ."

". . . I'll tell him as soon as I have a chance," Pete replied in a no-nonsense voice. "He left town last night and he isn't back yet, but I'll see that he gets your note—one way or another." He straightened and waved her on, much as a traffic cop would do. "Have a good trip."

Gwen, who was still stunned after hearing of Lance's absence, managed to nod and drive off. She reached the arterial and set her course for the freeway before even checking to see if Stanton Brown's car might be following. She heaved a heartfelt sigh of relief at discovering that she'd apparently escaped his net—if he'd ever cast one.

But as far as nets went, she hadn't accomplished much in trying to lower one over Lance's stubborn head. Although why that fact should bother her was still a mystery. Especially since he was such a mass of contradictions. He was tall and nice-looking, but she'd known men far more handsome who didn't raise her pulse rate a single beat. Lance possessed a deep, pleasant voice that could make a woman's knees go weak, but it was countered by a gray-eyed glance that could freeze a person like a midwestern winter. For a man whose career consisted of lounging around the swimming pool and endorsing paychecks from a well-heeled uncle, he had an ego that was indestructible and an assurance like reinforced steel. A woman would be a fool to tangle with him in a love affair.

Some love affair! she thought wryly, keeping a steady pace as the highway turned into a freeway on-ramp going east. Lance hadn't kissed her, hadn't whispered an endearment, or given her one compliment to remember. And unless he managed to come back to Palm Springs by the time she returned from Phoenix, she was going to have a lonely time by the swimming pool. It was a good thing that they'd taken a six months' lease on the villa because the way things were going, she'd need every bit of it!

Chapter Eight

Only four days elapsed before Gwen was retracing the long drive.

After arriving in Arizona, she'd reassured Louisa that Dennis and his betrothed weren't going to remain incommunicado forever—saying quite truthfully that from what she knew of Sherry, there was never a less likely person to desert the main stream of life.

That declaration, along with Pearl's avowal that she'd thought Sherry "a charming person," made Dennis' mother eventually decide that she'd be more comfortable recuperating from the shock in her Rancho Mirage home.

Gwen had hidden a grin, helped her pack the luggage, and turned the car back toward Palm Springs. Since the temperature was in the nineties both places, she was able to confirm that Louisa would probably do equally well in the southern California desert resort.

When they finally dropped her at the Carlton menage in nearby Rancho Mirage and made sure the housekeeper was on duty, Gwen transferred her aunt to the front seat of the car and drove off, saying, "If Louisa invites us to a reception when the happy couple finally reappear, I'm going to be a little late or come up with a sick headache."

"She has been a trifle wearing these past days," Pearl admitted. "Poor dear, she'll have to find another interest. Dennis has occupied her whole mind for so long."

"There are always tropical fish or guinea pigs."

"You sound almost as depressed as Louisa. Maybe it's this afternoon heat. I'm glad we started early enough this morning to miss most of it." Pearl gazed at her thoughtfully as Gwen concentrated on the traffic along East Canyon Drive. "What happened after I left? Lance was terribly close-mouthed when he called—" She broke off as the car swerved, adding, "Heavens that was close! Didn't you see that woman's turn signal?"

"Not soon enough," Gwen admitted. "I'm sorry. At least we had room to spare. You mentioned Lance—I didn't know he called you in Arizona. How did he know your number?"

"He said that he filched it from your telephone pad." Her aunt smiled slightly. "I was flattered. He has such nice manners."

Gwen thought of a few times when his manners hadn't been exemplary but she didn't mention them. "He must have had a reason for calling besides . . ."

"Buttering me up?" Pearl's amused tone showed that she hadn't missed that possibility either. "He certainly did, but since Dennis' phone call had already precipitated one crisis, I didn't have to bother to stage another one."

"I don't understand."

"Lance wanted you out of Palm Springs and under supervision. Naturally he thought of me."

"Good Lord, he's beyond belief! As if I couldn't take care of myself."

"Darling, when I heard of all that had happened to you, I'm not surprised. And when he said that he wasn't going to be around to watch over you . . ." Pearl shrugged. "I was glad that I had a legitimate excuse to get you to Phoenix."

Gwen's hands tightened on the steering wheel. "And I was happy to help you with Louisa—you know that. It's just that Lance can be so infuriating. Why didn't he stick around here himself? Probably he'd been invited to a posh house party and didn't want to disappoint his hostess."

"I doubt that. In his job, he doesn't have time for that sort of thing," Pearl said, reaching for her purse to find the case for her sunglasses.

"Managing three houses? That's absurd! Why, he even has help for the outdoor work. Somebody named Pete—I met him before I left."

Her aunt looked up from her search. "But this isn't Lance's regular job. I thought you knew. Louisa told me. Apparently he's the friend of a friend—something like that."

"Told you what?" Fortunately there was a stop-

151

light at that juncture so Gwen was able to confront the older woman.

"He's a very highly respected mining consultant. Always being sent off to places like Cornwall and Tasmania to check company explorations." Pearl gestured slightly. "The signal's changed to green."

Her last remark was accompanied by a honk from a van behind them. Gwen grimaced apologetically and started up again. "I don't understand. If he does things like that, what's he doing skimming a swimming pool in Palm Springs?"

"I think he owns it." Her aunt wasn't able to hide her amusement. "Anyhow, Louisa says that his uncle manages the Villas most of the time. Apparently, he's a charming man, too."

"How nice. It must run in the family," Gwen retorted wryly. She turned left off the Drive when she finally reached their familiar intersection, trying to keep her attention on necessities despite Pearl's latest disclosure. Hearing about Lance's true occupation was the final indignity to the day. She was painfully aware of the comments she'd made, fearing he was sensitive about a job that he'd attained only through his uncle's good nature. Lance must have had a hard time to keep from laughing in her face.

"He's surely back by now," Pearl continued, showing a knowledge of Lance's itinerary as well. "Would you like to invite him over for something cool before dinner? Sitting around the pool sounds delightful after so many hours in this car."

"I'm not sure that I feel much like socializing at this point," Gwen said as she finally pulled into the drive and braked in front of the villa. She turned off the ignition and opened her door, stretching gingerly as she got out of the car. "You go on in the house and I'll bring the luggage."

"You shouldn't struggle with it in this heat. Why not leave it in the trunk for now? We can transfer it later, once the sun has gone down." The older woman had located her door key and started up the walk. "Thank heavens for that breeze. At least it's cooler here than in Phoenix."

"All the more reason for you to sit on the side of the swimming pool."

"But what about you, dear?" Pearl asked as her niece hung back from the front steps.

"I'm not up to making conversation right now. It's open house every time we set foot on the patio here." In trying to think of a plausible excuse, Gwen's glance lit on an advertising brochure which had been left on the doorstep. She picked up the pamphlet and waved it triumphantly. "Just the place!"

"What in the world are you talking about?"

"Palm Canyon. I've heard about it and it isn't far from town."

"You mean you're going there *now?* After driving all day?" Pearl noted the weariness on Gwen's face and patted her cheek. "At least come in and change first," she coaxed, thinking that once her niece was in the house, she could be convinced to abandon this latest aberration. "We don't have to entertain now— maybe Lance isn't even here."

"I couldn't care less," Gwen announced, annoyed that she hadn't been successful with her red herring.

"Stanton Brown's car is parked over there and I don't want to talk to him either."

"Well, I hope *not*. He was the reason that Lance wanted you out of town in the first place."

"At this point, I'm thoroughly sick of hearing what Lance Fletcher wants or doesn't want." Gwen looked down at her red cotton sundress and decided that its wrinkles wouldn't matter to the Agua Caliente Indians who owned Palm Canyon, "I promise I'll come back in a better mood. And I would like to get a few pictures of the Canyon. It's hard to tell how long I can stay here, and it would be absurd to go home without taking my camera out of the case."

Pearl ignored most of that, saying in a concerned tone, "my dear, you're not going to cut your holiday short?"

"I don't know for sure." Which was putting it mildly, Gwen thought. She *did* know that she wasn't going to stay draped at the edge of the swimming pool on the off chance that Lance would stop by between trips. She dropped a quick kiss on Pearl's cheek and turned back toward the car. "I'll phone Montana tonight and learn what's going on. What's the use of having a good ranch foreman if he doesn't report now and then?"

"Then you won't be long—out at the canyon, I mean?"

Gwen shook her head. "The sun's too low for taking any decent pictures, but I can scout out the possibilities for another visit."

"At least it should be cooler at this time of the afternoon," Pearl told her. "When I was there in the middle of the day, there wasn't a breath of air down between those rocky canyon walls." As Gwen started to get in the car, Pearl added worriedly, "Don't you want to come in and change shoes, at least? Those sandals aren't practical for where you're going."

Gwen stared down at her high heels and then shrugged. "I won't be walking any distance, so it won't matter. If I don't get started, I'll have to abandon the whole idea. Don't wait dinner—I'll find something in the refrigerator when I come back."

Pearl watched the car disappear down the drive and chewed unhappily on her lower lip. She loved Gwen dearly but was wise enough to know that running away—even on as short a trip as Palm Canyon—wasn't going to solve her dilemma. Nor was there much hope from the other side. Even if Lance were home again, she couldn't very well go up and announce, "Gwen is either going to disappear back home or spend the rest of her vacation avoiding you unless you make her change her mind." He wouldn't thank her for such interference, and if Gwen heard about it, she'd probably leave for the north without even stopping to eat dinner first.

It wasn't easy to just sit by while two nice people resolutely snarled up their lives. Pearl decided that as she walked into the welcome cool and quiet of the villa. That decision also made her forego a temptation to stretch out on the comfortable couch and close her eyes for a few minutes. Instead she marched to the telephone and dialed a number which she'd found penciled on the pad the day they'd arrived. She heard it ringing and crossed her fingers. When a familiar voice answered, she uncrossed them triumphantly, saying, "Lance? What a pleasant surprise! This is Pearl Harris. No, I'm not calling from Phoenix—we got back a few minutes ago. I wondered if Chen could accommodate one more for dinner tonight? That will be lovely—thank you. No, I don't think Gwen can make it. She isn't here now and I'm not sure when she'll be back." There was a pause then while Pearl listened to Lance's apology for the oath he'd just uttered. She interrupted to say, "That's all right—it was my reaction, too. Especially when I learned she was going to such an isolated place by herself—" She broke off again when Lance cut in and then replied, "Coffee now? At your place? Yes, of course. I'll be right over."

She hung up and nodded with satisfaction as she headed toward the front hall. The conversation had gone just as she hoped. One couldn't interfere but one could certainly nudge events in the proper direction, she told herself. With any luck, things might turn out right after all.

While Pearl's strategic maneuvering was going on, Gwen was driving back toward the city center and looking for the turnoff from Palm Canyon Drive which, according to the brochure on the seat beside her, led directly to the Agua Caliente Indian Reservation and their famed canyon sites. Apparently there was a nominal entrance fee to the reservation but not because of tribal need. It was well publicized that the Indians were the largest single landowner in the Palm Springs area. By leasing just ten and a half miles of their reservation for development, each of the 150 natives had become millionaires, and there was no end of the largesse in sight.

When Gwen finally turned onto the road marked for Palm Canyon, she wasn't surprised to find it lined with expensive housing developments. By then she had become accustomed to seeing acres of homes featuring North African architecture located just beyond another elegant tract specializing in Mission Spanish or Southern Colonial. As she continued down the two-lane road, however, the residences thinned and finally disappeared—leaving the gray, unadorned desert to provide the ultimate contrast.

A simple fence marked another reservation boundary a little later, but a tiny gatehouse with an Indian woman occupying most of it was the only evidence of officialdom. She accepted Gwen's entrance fee after announcing that no visitors would be admitted after four o'clock. "That's when I close this gate," she stated pleasantly but firmly. "You won't have much time to see things."

Gwen murmured something and drove on down the one-way gravel road. It wasn't until she'd gone a short distance that she realized she should have asked if the exit gate was locked at four o'clock, too, or if visitors already in the reservation were given a grace period for departure. She sighed and drove on, not wanting to waste valuable time looking for a place to turn around so she could go back and check with the gatekeeper.

One thing was sure—any vision she'd had of relaxing for an hour or so in solitude was a lost cause. She'd just have to try for a few pictures in Palm Canyon, which a leaning signpost proclaimed to be straight ahead, and then go on back. She looked around the reservation land on either side of her and shuddered at the thought of having to spend the night in such a desolate place.

The only company she'd have would be boulders and what looked to be prickly gray underbrush. She rolled down the car window as far as possible to get all the air she could in the car and turned off the air-conditioner. The breeze felt as if she'd opened an oven door, but it was better to become accustomed to it gradually than to get it in one blast when she finally stopped and stepped outside.

Ahead of the car, a grove of tall palm trees loomed out of the stark desert scene and she knew that she was approaching the famed canyon where so many motion pictures had been shot.

At least she wouldn't have to worry about sharing the locale with any cameramen or visitors just then, she decided. There wasn't another vehicle or person in sight. In fact, there hadn't been any signs of human habitation except for a ramshackle van parked near the gatehouse. Hardly the kind for a tribal millionaire to drive, she thought, trying to visualize the ticket lady behind the steering wheel and then abandoning the fantasy.

Gwen was aware that she was thinking about such things because the solitude of the Canyon was a little more overpowering than she'd contemplated. At that moment, she would have been glad to encounter even a jackrabbit along the roadside, but the animals had apparently decided to take cover from the heat as well as everyone else.

"Mad dogs and Englishmen," she reflected and

looked for a wide spot in the road where she could pull off. Not that it really mattered; she had the whole darned reservation to herself!

She remained behind the wheel for a moment after she'd turned off the ignition, looking at the lush ribbon of growth which resulted from a stream at the bottom of the canyon. A quick check of the publicity brochure revealed that the palms which gave the canyon its name were the *Washingtonia Filifera* variety. The booklet went on to say that there was a fifteen-mile length of wilderness and used adjectives like rough, barren, and desertlike to describe it. They could also have used sweltering and bleak, Gwen thought, and wished she'd chosen an air-conditioned part of Palm Springs to lick her wounds.

The very core of the canyon down the short trail to her left was beautiful, she told herself, knowing that she should walk down to the stream and try for a picture of lengthening shadows on the surrounding rocks. Reluctantly she reached for her camera on the back seat and opened the car door. After another look at the deserted countryside, she left her purse tucked under the front seat of the car and set out.

It was only a yard or two before she stopped, grimaced with annoyance, and went back to the car. Her aunt had been right; flimsy strap sandals with high heels were ridiculous in the surroundings. If she didn't break an ankle wearing them down the path to the stream, she'd certainly scratch the heels beyond repair. She undid the straps and slipped out of them, putting the shoes on the hood of the car—a bright red beacon in the drab surroundings. "To lead me home," Gwen murmured and smiled at the incongruous picture they made.

At least she'd been sensible enough to go barelegged since she'd gotten a passable tan. She started down the steep rocky path to the stream again, clambering carefully over the rounded boulders. As she went from one to another, she told herself that it wasn't the right time of day for snakes to emerge from their retreats. It was a ridiculous assumption and she knew it. She also knew that a pair of red sandals wouldn't have helped a bit in a confrontation with a rattler or a sidewinder. Her only hope was that there'd been so many tourists stomping down the trail that any self-respecting snake would have left the neighborhood months before.

That argument sounded more logical. Gwen scrambled over another warm, smooth rock and surveyed the dirt track winding down from it before dropping onto the fine gravel surface. A minute or so later, she reached the edge of the stream bed.

She stood motionless, warily surveying the quiet oasis. Then, she moved a few feet along the bank of the shallow waterway and leaned against a huge boulder, relaxing as its stored warmth from the sun soothed her tense shoulder muscles.

The stream made a rippling noise as it slipped over and down around the rocks scattered in its bed. To Gwen it was the pleasantest part of the whole place, because the palm grove which lined the banks was almost forbidding. The shaggy fronds of the trees were so dense overhead that they cut out the clear sky and the sunlight. That gave the only air in the sheltered canyon pocket a hot dusty breath prompting Gwen to reach down for a handful of cool water to splash over her face.

It helped a little—enough that she dried her hands on the flounce of her sundress and set about looking for a decent picture angle. She wasn't anywhere near professional caliber but possessed enough sense to know that composition and lighting were important. That meant she had to climb over some more rocks to get the setting she wanted, one that had a maximum amount of the lush oasis and just enough barren hill-side for contrast.

Engrossed in her task, she forgot all about possible snakes, and the two unattractive insects she'd avoided on her way down. She *was* aware of some gray mourning doves with their low throaty voices, plus a type of wren living in the palms which she resolved to identify in a bird guide once she returned to the villa. The birds were fluttering about on a flat rock near the stream edge and she advanced slowly, trying to reach a place with decent lighting without disturbing her subjects.

When she finally managed, she put the camera to her eye to readjust the focus. An instant later—to her dismay—the birds in the viewfinder scattered and disappeared in a flurry of wings and dust. "Damn!" Gwen said, lowering her camera in disgust.

"I'm sorry about that," came a man's voice behind her. "Did I ruin your picturetaking?"

Gwen whirled, almost losing her footing in the soft, damp sand of the creek edge. Her surprise was so great that it took a moment for her to properly identify the man standing just six feet away. "Mr. Brown! I didn't know you were here." She looked up through the palm trunks toward the roadway. "I didn't see your car."

"It's not far away." Sherry's employer gestured casually back toward the trail. He looked longingly at a smooth boulder beside him but after running an investigative finger along its surface and noting the gritty dust, he appeared to discard it as a possible resting place. Instead he took an immaculate handkerchief from his gabardine slacks and blotted his broad forehead, looking almost resentfully at their surroundings. "You're a difficult person to run down, Miss Lawson."

Gwen rubbed her palms on her cotton skirt to dry them. It was necessary before putting her camera back in the case, and just then, it seemed important to keep her movements brisk and natural. "Why should you want to run me down?"

Despite her resolution, her voice must have wavered on the last words. Stanton Brown's pudgy hand waved deprecatingly before he pushed the handkerchief back in his pocket. "Oh, not literally, Miss Lawson. That was a bad choice of words on my part. I just meant that I've been wanting to get together with you. Then I find that you've left the state for a few days. At first I thought you'd gone with Sherry—" He put up his hand again when she would have interrupted. "No, I realize now that you didn't have anything to do with her abrupt departure. I understand it was true love. Touching, isn't it?"

The solid set of his jaw belied any reason for Gwen to believe him. She tried to assume an innocent expression which she hoped wasn't too imbecilic. "All I know is that Dennis' mother was floored by the news of their engagement and pretty unhappy that she couldn't tell them in person. My aunt thinks that they probably won't surface until long after the honeymoon." Put *that* bit of news out on your grapevine, Mr. Brown, she added silently.

"Is that why you came back today?" he asked after a perceptible pause.

She managed to look confused at that without trying. "Heavens, no! My aunt wanted to spend the rest of her holiday in Palm Springs, not Phoenix. It didn't affect me one way or the other."

"Oh, come now, Miss Lawson—don't try the meek little woman bit. A few weeks ago you might have convinced me. That's when I still thought that your aunt possessed the controlling interest in your family holdings. It took a while before I learned differently." He broke off to stare upward in annoyance, as if wishing he could decree that the sun disappear, instead of shining directly on his thinning pate. "I don't know why in hell you chose this hotbox for your first afternoon back in town."

"Because I wanted some peace and quiet," she told him frankly. "And to be alone for a while."

"Not to avoid a discussion with me?"

She didn't even try to avoid his accusing gaze. The sooner she convinced him, the sooner he'd leave. "I'm telling you the unvarnished truth. I haven't the foggiest idea where Dennis and Sherry are holed up. If he wouldn't tell his own mother, he certainly wasn't spreading the news around."

A fleeting frown went over Brown's perspiring face as he reached for the handkerchief again. "I don't give a damn about that blonde. Or that mama's boy she's hitched onto. They've both outlived their usefulness so far as I'm concerned." For the first time, his expression took on a vestige of humor. "Your friend Dennis will need a fat line of credit if he hopes to hang onto her. Sherry has expensive tastes."

"Maybe she'll reform," Gwen said, trying to keep the conversation in lighter channels. "Love's supposed to work miracles."

"It didn't work for Carlton." Stanton Brown's eyes resumed their basilisk stare. "He told me he was going to marry you. It would have been easier to deal with him—that's why I held off for so long."

"Held off?" she repeated faintly, wondering if the heat was getting to her. "What did Dennis have to do with you, for pete's sake?"

He waved that aside brusquely. "I'm not here to answer questions. The only thing I want to talk about is that parcel of property you own on the Canadian border. The one that I thought belonged to the old lady—" At Gwen's sudden scowl he rephrased the last two words. ". . . to your aunt. Sherry was the one who figured out the mixup in names."

"That was when she met Dennis, I suppose."

"You're right about that. Not that she noised it around. I just heard that she was dealing with a local real estate man who had an inside track to that property. Some track," Brown said sardonically. "I wasted weeks before I found out that he was just talking big about marrying you. When he got down here, I pointed it out."

His level droning tone sent the first stirrings of fear through Gwen's body. It was impulse rather than considered thought which made her blurt out, "Then that night he was run off the road wasn't an accident?"

Brown's straggly eyebrows went up in mock dismay. "What's the beef? Nobody was hurt. It was just a reminder for Carlton to be more careful next time when he dealt with me."

"And what about my aunt? I suppose she didn't count."

"Mrs. Harris doesn't figure in my plans." He brushed a minute piece of grit from his thumbnail as if it were of major importance. "As I said before, my business is with you at this point—nobody else. I'll meet any reasonable price for that property of yours. Cash on the barrelhead with a bonus for making up your mind in a hurry. I've waited too long already."

She stared at him, scarcely able to believe her ears. "But I don't *want* to sell my land. It's been in our family since the territory was settled."

Stanton Brown's lips clamped into a straight line. "That's why I preferred to deal with Carlton when I thought he was going to marry you. He wouldn't have bothered with such sentimental hogwash."

"Just because a woman gets married—"

"I haven't time for philosophical discussions, and this sure as hell isn't the place for one." He shot another angry glance toward the sunlit sky before focusing back on her. "What kind of money would make you change your mind?"

"The property's not for sale, Mr. Brown." Gwen tried to sound as dignified as possible, considering that she was standing barefoot in a creek bed.

"That's it, period. Now, if you don't mind, I'd like to get back to town."

He put out a pudgy hand. While he didn't actually touch her, his expression was so threatening that Gwen stopped immediately, making no attempt to brush past him.

"I intend to have that property one way or another," he said. "If you're going to be difficult, then I'll just have to show you I mean business. And I know lots of ways to do that. Ask your friend Dennis about it when he gets in touch. It won't do you any good to ask Sherry—she knows enough to keep her mouth shut."

"You actually think that threatening me will—"

"You're not dealing with a cheap hood," he warned, cutting her off in midsentence again. "It won't do you a damn bit of good to complain to the cops or your lawyer. If you don't deal with me, you'll regret it. Things happen."

She had to clear her throat before she could get the words out to ask, "What sort of things?"

He smiled but there wasn't a trace of humor in his heavy-lidded eyes. "Who can say? There are lots of accidents that never get reported—like the hole in your stair carpet. Now that could have had serious consequences. Or Carlton running off the road—that shows what could happen any night in a car. And don't forget, your aunt could be a real responsibility with such frail health. Think about that, Miss Lawson —then we'll talk again. I'll be around for the rest of the week." He started to leave but turned back to ask, "Can I help you to your car?"

It was hard for Gwen to keep from shuddering.

"No, thanks," she said curtly. "I'll be a little longer."

"As you wish. Keep in mind what I said."

Gwen had to hang onto the big stream boulder to keep her knees from sagging as reaction set in after Stanton Brown left. He made his way back up the rocky trail with a surprisingly fast pace for such a heavy man. She felt a small bit of satisfaction as she saw him stumble going over the last piece of overhang before joining his chauffeur on the shoulder of the road. Not surprisingly, the ubiquitous Max was in full uniform, despite the temperature.

Gwen waited until she heard their car start and get well away before she dashed up the trail herself. All the dangers she'd worried about on the way down were forgotten in the light of this last, bigger threat. And despite Stanton Brown's warning, she was heading straight to the villa for help!

She pulled up when she finally reached the top of the steep path, breathing hard and clutching her side. She checked to note if her car were still where she'd left it and felt an indescribable relief at seeing the familiar outline. Then she shook her head as if to clear it; why on earth should she think that Stanton Brown would resort to car theft or vandalism? Obviously he fancied himself in a more elevated category.

Gwen rubbed a hand over her hot forehead and started toward the car, limping on the sharp gravel at the roadside. By then, the bottoms of her feet felt as if she'd been walking on razor blades. At least the soles of her shoes would offer some protection on the drive home.

That thought made her aware of something that

had puzzled her every since her first glimpse of the car. She was sure she'd left the sandals on the hood. She might be suffering from overexposure to the sun and a surfeit of Stanton Brown, but she definitely remembered that final silly gesture.

She wanted to hurry, to dash to the car and see if Max or his boss had put the sandals inside, but her tender feet kept her from it. She managed to hobble along the last yards, carefully avoiding the sharper bits of gravel or she'd have finished on her hands and knees.

Her first anxious glimpse through the tightly closed car window brought a smile. There they were! Two familiar bright red sandals placed squarely in the middle of the front seat.

And then her relieved expression faded like the sun which was disappearing behind the gray rocky hill at the canyon's edge. For someone had neatly placed her purse beside the shoes on the seat and then, with a sense of the dramatic, her car key ring was left next to that.

Gwen shut her eyes slowly and opened them again but nothing had changed; the car was securely and efficiently locked. Everything she needed was inside beyond her reach, and she was stranded in a deserted Indian reservation where the gate was now closed for the night.

Stanton Brown hadn't wasted any time in making his point!

Chapter Nine

In the first awful moments of her predicament, Gwen had visions of herself on the glide path to oblivion, withering away in the hot desert breeze like a sponge taken out of water, abandoned like a desiccated lump.

Her first reaction was to sit down beside the car—to take advantage of it as a windbreak, at least. However, it wasn't long before she realized that, while the place looked deserted, there was a considerable insect population in residence to refute that theory. Bare legs and a wide-skirted sundress didn't help and she scrambled up again, brushing two ants from her ankle in the process. Being abandoned was bad enough without providing a free lunch for all the creepy-crawlies in the neighborhood.

It was about then that her panic lessened and common sense returned. Even if the Indian woman at the gate had quit for the day, Pearl wouldn't be quite so casual about an empty place at the dinner table. It would be just a matter of time after that before her aunt corralled young Pete or Chen to drive her to the rescue. Possibly even Lance himself, Gwen hazarded, if he were back in town.

Another venturesome ant started up her instep and she vigorously brushed it off. It was one thing to think about eventual rescue, but for the moment she'd have to take some kind of evasive action.

A glance around the deserted landscape showed lengthening shadows and absolutely nothing else. The canyon was at least three or four miles from the entrance; it was out of the question to try and hike back with bare feet. Which meant staying by the car. And if she couldn't sit on the ground—it left only sitting on the car.

That was the way that Lance eventually found her an hour later; sitting in lotus position on the hood, looking like a very unusual yogi with the skirt of her bright red sundress wrapped around her legs.

Gwen continued to sit there, apprehensive and wide-eyed, until his car braked beside hers with a flurry of gravel and she recognized her rescuer. But before she could scramble down from her perch and proclaim her relief, he announced angrily, "I'll be damned if you don't get in more trouble than any woman I've ever known! If you keep on this way, we'll both be old before our time. You aren't hurt, are you?" The last came as he reached up and pulled her unceremoniously to the ground beside him.

"No—no, of course not," Gwen said, still dazed by his reception.

"Well, then why in the devil are you sitting here?" He leaned over to brush dust from her wrinkled skirt and took in her bare feet for the first time. "My God! This isn't the place to run around without shoes. What have you done with them?"

"They're right there in the front seat," Gwen said in an ominously level tone. "Beside my car keys."

Lance's angry face changed almost comically as he took in her predicament, and a crooked grin replaced the stern line of his mouth. "At least we won't have to worry about managing two cars. You don't have an extra key?"

"Do you think I'd still be here if I had a choice?"

"I wasn't sure when I drove up. You looked as if you were practicing to be a guru. Hey—hold still! I'll carry you to my car. You can't walk around like that."

She reached up and put her arms around his neck with a sigh of relief when he bent to lift her. "I won't argue. You know, I've never felt so helpless in my life. I may never take my shoes off again."

"It's probably just as well you did. Otherwise, you'd have had a terrible walk back to the gate." He put her down beside his car and started to open the door. "After this though you'd better carry a duplicate set of keys if you're prone to this sort of thing."

She hung back when he would have urged her in. "I'm not to blame. That so and so of a Stanton Brown or his Max deliberately locked me out of my car. I can't wait to give him a piece of my mind." She sneezed violently in the middle of her sentence. "And maybe a cold, too."

"That's just the dust around here," Lance said, shoving her onto the front seat without further delay so he could get behind the wheel. "Are you serious? I mean, about Brown leaving you out here on purpose?"

"What does it take to convince you? I'd have to be ready for a cotton box to manage this!"

"Well, not many women would go haring off after driving eight hours on the freeway. If your aunt hadn't phoned me, you could have been stuck out here for hours. Just be thankful she has more . . ." he broke off, as if realizing that he was getting in dangerous territory again.

"Sense. Go on—you can say it. I'd be the first to agree." Gwen watched him start the car and struggle to make a U-turn on the narrow track.

"Then why did you do such a damned silly thing? You must have known I was waiting to see you at home."

Gwen wanted to say that was exactly the reason that she'd come to Palm Canyon, that she'd needed time to become accustomed to the new Lance whom her aunt had revealed; a man with an impressive career and apparently an equally impressive bank account. She'd lost her heart to him in his old guise, but his new background left her shy and uncertain.

Lance mistook her silence. He reached out for her hand and pulled it against his thigh. "I'm sorry—you've gone through hell and all I do is shout at you."

"You can do that all you want. I knew that Aunt Pearl would send out an SOS, but what really scared me was the possibility that Stanton Brown would come back and try some more persuasion."

"You don't have to worry about that ape any longer." Lance was concentrating on the potholes in the road but there was a ring of authority in his voice.

"But I do," she almost wailed. "He's the one responsible for the hole in the stair carpet and Dennis' accident—there was even somebody who went through my things when I first arrived. I'm sure of it."

"So am I."

"And it's going to get even worse. He warned me about that—" Her voice broke off as Lance's quiet comment sunk in. "What did you say?"

"That Brown was responsible for all the trouble. I suspected it at the time. That's why I wanted you out of town while I went to Los Angeles and tried to clip his wings."

It was all coming too fast for Gwen. She did manage to note that the gate through which she'd entered the reservation was closed and barred as they came upon it. Lance took to a dirt shoulder around a break in the fence, not slackening his speed.

"And all the time I thought you just couldn't wait to see the back of me. After everything that had happened that day," she said in meek tones, very unlike her normal self.

The difference didn't go unnoticed. Lance's mouth quirked with amusement as he replied, "I admit that I didn't give a very good account of myself, but after that episode up in the tram parking lot, I knew I couldn't take any more chances."

"I—don't—quite understand what you mean," she said carefully.

"Then you *are* missing some cylinders, but we can get to that later." He shot a glance at his watch. "There isn't time now."

Gwen saw her golden dreams start to fade. "Why not? What's the rush?"

"I want to get you home."

"But I'm fine. Aside from a few bites," she scratched her ankle and then reached for her shoes. "I'd better put these on."

"Do that. Otherwise, I'll have you at my mercy, too." He pretended to twirl a waxed mustache.

"At least there's pavement around here. It was the gravel road that left me stranded."

"There must be a moral to that."

"There is. Something about not insulting the alligator until you've climbed out of the river." Her glance turned anxious again. "Were you serious when you said that Stanton Brown couldn't cause any more trouble? Because he really wants some land that I own."

"Forget it. He's going to be too busy staying out of the hoosegow for any real estate ventures. The authorities picked him up an hour or so ago."

"But why? I haven't even filed a complaint—" Gwen began.

"They had some others. I found that out when I went in to Los Angeles and checked with a friend of mine in the DEA."

"The what?"

"Drug Enforcement Agency. Brown was implicated in a big marijuana bust on the Washington coast a few months ago but they couldn't make the charges stick. When Sherry mentioned to me that he was interested in border property in Montana, that sounded as if he was bringing in contraband along the British Columbia coast and needed a way to slip it down to the States."

She whistled softly. "I can see where the authorities would be interested in hearing about *that*. But I still don't see how they could pick him up on just suspicion—he'll be back on the street operating in no time."

"It wasn't the DEA that arrested him—it was Internal Revenue. They'd been gathering evidence on income tax evasion for months. This time the noose is tight. And Sherry's willing to make it tighter. Or so Pete reported."

"Your gardener?" Gwen put her hands up to her head as if to hold it on. "Good Lord! Next you'll be telling me that Chen works for the CIA."

"Not a chance. Chen's a firm believer in private enterprise."

"But Pete . . ." Gwen broke off to say, "I didn't think he was a gardener—"

"He'll be crushed. I'll have to tell him to pull a few weeds next time."

She waved that aside. "You mean he was watching Stanton Brown as an undercover man?"

Lance took his attention from the traffic to check his watch again. "Actually, he was watching you. I didn't want you to have any more 'accidents' while I was away. It was a great relief when Pearl convinced you to go to Arizona."

"She finally admitted that was a set-up job."

"You be nice to her!" he said with mock sternness. "She's been on my side all the way along and I needed all the help I could get. Especially when I found out that it was *your* real estate up on the border." He stopped for a traffic light near the turnoff to the Villas and bestowed a quelling look. "It wasn't until today that she told me how big that ranch of yours really is."

Gwen didn't attempt to evade his unspoken accusation. "I didn't want to put you off. At the time, I thought you just wandered around swimming pools. You didn't mention that it was *your* swimming pool either."

"I didn't think it mattered then."

He started up again, but they'd turned toward the Villas before she summoned the courage to ask, "And what about later?"

"It mattered too much. I could see that you'd pegged me for living from one remittance check to the next."

"That didn't bother me so much," she confessed. "At the beginning, I suspected it was one blonde to the next. And you can stop grinning like a Cheshire cat—I've been miserable."

"Well, from now on you can stop worrying," he said, turning into the driveway and beeping gently on the horn as they pulled up in front of her house. "Stanton Brown's out of circulation. All you and Pearl have to do is enjoy the sunshine and tell Chen what to cook for dinner for the next week or so."

She stared at him, perplexed, only vaguely aware of her aunt's welcoming figure in the doorway. "What are *you* going to be doing all that time?"

176

He reached across to open her car door, pausing just long enough to deposit a light kiss on the tip of her nose before he straightened again behind the steering wheel. "If I don't catch the San Francisco plane that leaves twenty minutes from now to connect with the Anchorage flight after that and the Nome flight after that, the people I work for will be mighty disagreeable. And while I wouldn't have minded taking a remittance check from my relatives, I'm sure as hell not going to take one from my wife. So get out of here"—he gave her a gentle shove as he spoke—"and let me go earn a living."

She stood on the parking strip and managed to close the car door but hung onto it for support, murmuring dazedly, "You did say wife?"

His grin took at least ten years from his age as he started to ease the car away. "That I did. I'll be in touch. We'll discuss it then."

Gwen had ten long days to think about Lance's abrupt proposal. Fortunately, her aunt was around to soothe her impatience, confiding that Lance had very properly announced his intentions early on. And when Gwen complained mildly that someone might have given her a hint, Pearl looked down her nose to say, "I wouldn't have dreamed of interfering," before going off to phone Louisa and report on this latest happy development.

Stanton Brown and Max disappeared from the landscape as if they'd never existed. One night at dinner, Chen reported briefly that their belongings had been removed from the villa. After that, he'd served a special dessert, effectively shutting off any further discussion on the former tenants.

However, the cook proved that he wasn't so reticent on other matters. He came pounding over to Gwen's villa the very next morning, bearing a special delivery package which he thrust into her hands, beaming like a proud father all the while.

Inside there was an airline ticket to Haines, Alaska, for the next day; a house key with an address clipped to it; and a magnificent emerald-cut diamond engagement ring in a black velvet box. There was also a note in Lance's bold hand that said, "Want to talk about it now?"

Gwen showed the note to her aunt and Chen (although it wasn't necessary since they'd both already read it over her shoulder). "Imagine! Thinking I'd just come running! I like that!"

Pearl sighed in a way that showed she hadn't forgotten what it was like to be young at heart. "So do I," she breathed. "Are you all packed?"

Gwen nodded and tucked the ring carefully into her purse, thinking that it wouldn't be long until Lance put it on her finger. "I have been for days," she confessed.

It took four different airplanes and a long taxi ride before she finally approached her destination. Her very first glimpse revealed it would have been hard to find a greater contrast to the Desert Villas in Palm Springs. She'd left bleak desert hillsides against a pale blue sky and come north to lush, green mountain scenery with snowcapped peaks. They loomed against a sky so blue that the color might have spilled from a tube of pure cobalt. The sunlit waters of the Lynn Canal were in front of her when the taxi ground to a stop in front of a magnificent A-frame dwelling almost hidden in the trees. After paying off the driver, Gwen unlocked the front door and stared, entranced, around her.

It was a superb structure that fitted into the rugged surroundings as if it had been part of an inspired master plan. There was a massive stone fireplace, a spiral stairway which led to balcony sleeping quarters, and a modern kitchen gleaming with touches of copper and birch. But best of all were the mammoth windows at the front of the living room, overlooking the busy canal where a sleek, blue-hulled Alaska ferry kept company with three whales roaming northward. The mighty monsters proclaimed their presence with misty spouts of water from their blowholes, fascinating everything within sight.

It was such a wondrous panorama that Gwen kept her eyes on it as she changed out of her travel suit into jeans and loafers. Then she ran out onto the deck and down the trail to the edge of the canal for a closer look.

She was still whale-watching a half hour later when she heard the sound of a car in the quiet air. It was pure instinct which made her turn and dash for the lodge, forgetting to skirt a puddle on the path as she reached the steps of the deck. She squished up them, automatically noting a car parked nearby, and then slipped out of her damp loafers to keep from leaving wet tracks on the carpet.

Lance came out onto the deck just as she started for the door.

For an instant, they both stopped—hardly believing that finally their moment had come.

Gwen stared at his familiar tall figure as if she hadn't seen it for years and when his grin flashed, she felt a burst of joy so great that her heartbeat thundered in her ears. "I'm here," she announced breathlessly, unable for the life of her to manage anything better.

"So you are. And it's a damned good thing, too." Lance strode forward and yanked her into his arms, kissing her like a man hungry for the taste and feel of her. When he finally raised his head, he framed her radiant face between his palms and stared down at it. "Dear God, I couldn't have lasted much longer."

"That makes two of us. Do you know that's the very first time you've kissed me? Properly, I mean."

Laughter brimmed in his gray eyes, making Gwen wonder how she could ever have thought them cold. "I was saving myself for marriage," he said solemnly. "I don't believe in casual fly-by-night affairs."

"If that's so," she pulled the ring case from the pocket of her jeans and handed it to him. "Maybe you'd do the official honors."

It was slipped onto the proper finger without delay and Lance folded her even closer as he kissed her again, showing remarkable expertise for a man who claimed to be out of practice.

"I'm sorry I was late," he said, pressing another

soft kiss on her palm, "but I just flew in from the north and I stopped in town to find out about getting a marriage license. That is, if you'd like to have a honeymoon here." His expression was wry as he acknowledged, "You haven't had much of a chance for any 'druthers and that's certainly the bride's prerogative."

"You mean we really can stay in this marvelous place?"

"I've leased it from a friend of mine so we can stay as long as we want. Unfortunately, I could only wangle two weeks for a honeymoon right now but there's no reason you can't come with me when I fly north again."

"It sounds heavenly! There's only one thing—"

His brows met in a worried line. "If you're concerned about your ranch . . ."

"It's not that," she assured him. "The foreman's great and Aunt Pearl's promised to keep an eye on things, besides."

"Well, then . . ."

"I *do* think that somebody named Lancelot could have arrived on a white charger or something more romantic than a station wagon when he's proposing marriage."

His clasp didn't slacken but he winced visibly. "Dammit—nothing's sacred anymore! How did you find out about that?"

"I never reveal my secrets," she intoned and then grinned mischievously up at him. "It's all right— I'm not named Guinevere so you don't have to feel trapped."

"But I have been—ever since that afternoon I

found you wrestling with the umbrella." Lance's tone was whimsical but there was no hiding the darkening passion in his eyes. "For a little while, I didn't know what had hit me. I just remember inventing that job to keep you around—"

"Chen told us about his unexpected 'vacation.'"

He nodded sheepishly. "And I remember wanting to toss Dennis into the sagebrush every time he put a hand on you. But up in that tram lot, when you could have been killed pulling that youngster away from the car, I knew then that I'd fallen head over heels for you."

"So you snarled and almost took my head off when you left me at the door of the villa afterwards," she replied softly. "I know now that you were just trying to watch out for me."

"But then?"

"It doesn't matter, darling. I was head over heels in love with you, too. Unfortunately, you didn't stick around long enough to find out."

"Until now?"

"Until now," she agreed. Then, as he bent to pick up her loafers, she asked, "What in heaven's name are you doing?"

"Making sure that *you* stick around," he said, marching down the steps to deposit her shoes on the front seat of the station wagon and locking the car doors.

Gwen watched him come back up on the deck. "All that just so we can talk?" she asked provocatively when he was with her once again.

"Hell no! I'm through with talking," Lance said

in a decided tone as he put her arms around his neck, to carry her in the house.

Gwen smiled, brushed a soft kiss over his cheek, and leaned back to close the door firmly behind them as they crossed the threshold.

About the Author

Glenna Finley is a native of Washington State. She earned her degree from Stanford University in Russian Studies and in Speech and Dramatic Arts, with emphasis on radio.

After a stint in radio and publicity work in Seattle, she went to New York City to work for NBC as a producer in its international division. In addition, she worked with the "March of Time" and *Life* magazine.

As a producer, she had her own show about activities in Manhattan, a show that was broadcast to England. The programs were similar to those of the "Voice of America."

Though her life in New York was exciting, she eventually returned to the Northwest where she married. Currently residing in Seattle with her husband, Donald Witte, and their son, she loves to travel, and draws heavily on her travels and experiences for the novels that have been published. Her books for NAL have sold millions of copies.